Triple ˙ Creek

Ranch

Book One

Unbroken

Rebekah A. Morris (signature)

Rebekah A. Morris

Copyright © 2013 Rebekah A. Morris

All rights reserved.

ISBN: 1493657062
ISBN-13: 978-1493657063

Read Another Page Publishing

DEDICATION

To Christian Steffes and Grace Tallman who kept asking for the next part. Without their persistence this book would not be in your hands right now.

CONTENTS

1	The Letter	1
2	First Skirmish	9
3	Home	17
4	Mistress of Triple Creek	25
5	Encounters	33
6	The Smell of Trouble	41
7	Nothing to Wear	49
8	Poor Orlena	59
9	What Can She Do?	69
10	Setting Things Straight	77
11	Results of Temper	85
12	An Answered Prayer	95
13	Relief	105
14	Unexpected Tears	115
15	A Refreshing Interlude	125
16	The Wrong Shoes	133
17	Fresh Courage	143
18	Round-Up Plans	153
19	The Loneliest Times	161

20	"I'll Be Very Careful"	169
21	Unlatched Gates	177
22	Unexpected Results	187
23	Waiting	195
24	A Matter of Character	203
25	Partial Surrender	213

Chapter 1

THE LETTER

The blazing sun was well past mid day, and the air was hot and heavy. The fields were green with rows of fast drying hay turning golden brown. Soon it would be time to load the hay wagons, and Jenelle shook her head at the thought of the long, hot days before them. A knock on the door interrupted her thoughts and opening it she found a neighbor boy.

"Pa and I were just in town and picked up your mail for you, Mrs. Mavrich. Pa didn't think you'd be getting there this week."

Jenelle smiled. "Why thank you, Ted. I'm sure we won't. Not with Norman trying to get the fences fixed so they can move the horses. Tell your Pa we're much obliged."

Waving, Ted ran back to the wagon which was waiting for him at the end of the lane.

Thumbing quickly through the mail, Jenelle paused and looked at the last envelope with a frown.

"This looks important," she murmured dropping the rest of the mail on the table and stepping out into the heat.

"Norman," Jenelle called.

Norman looked up from the fence he was mending. Wiping the sweat from his face with his handkerchief, he straightened his back.

"This just came." Jenelle waved an envelope. "It looked

important, so I brought it out."

A quick glance at the postmark and Norman was tearing the letter open. Rapidly his eyes scanned it before he spoke.

"Grandmother is dead."

"Oh Norman," Jenelle's voice as well as her face was full of sympathy. "That letter is from—?"

"Her lawyer." His face grew perplexed.

"Is it your sister?" she asked softly.

"Yes."

"Well?"

Norman looked up from the hole his boot was making in the dust. "I'm her only kin. Darling, Orlena is only twelve, yet she was such a terror the last time I saw her, I'm almost afraid of her."

Jenelle didn't speak but waited in silence for her husband to continue.

"The lawyer says that she was in boarding school last year, but since I am now her legal guardian, I have to decide what to do with her." He sighed as though suddenly weary.

"Why don't we bring her here?"

"You aren't serious."

"I am. I've only met her once, but if what you say of her is true, she needs help. Can't we try to help her?"

"Sweetheart, you're an angel!" And he kissed her. "You know, don't you, Darling, that I have to go to the city for at least a few days to get Grandmother's affairs settled."

"And bring Orlena home," his wife added sweetly.

Norman smiled. "And that." He frowned thoughtfully at the fence post. "Let me finish this here and then I'll be in to make plans. You had best get in out of this sun." He gave Jenelle another kiss and returned to work.

Early the following morning found Norman and Jenelle at the station in town. The train would be leaving in a few minutes giving the couple time for a few last words of farewell.

Turning to his wife, Norman asked for the second time, "Are you sure you'll be all right with me gone?"

A light, merry laugh was her answer as she turned bright, blue eyes to meet the grey ones of her husband. "I'll be just fine. I won't worry about anything on the ranch except for the house and the chickens."

"That's right. Let Hardrich take care of the rest. He's the best foreman anyone could ask for. Uncle trained him well."

A warning whistle sounded from the train, and the conductor called, "All aboard!"

"I must go, Darling. Be careful driving home." Norman gave her a tender embrace and grabbed his valise. "I'll wire when I know what train I'm returning on. But," he called back to her as he stepped on the train, "have Hardrich meet me if you aren't feeling well."

Jenelle laughed and waved her handkerchief. Did he think she would really let the foreman drive to meet her returning husband? And sister? For a moment Jenelle paused wondering what that sister would be like.

With a blast of steam, a shriek of the whistle and a roar of the engine, the train moved off down the track toward that distant city, away, each second farther away, from the young and beautiful wife standing alone at the station waving her small white handkerchief. Turning slowly back to the light spring wagon after the train had disappeared, Jenelle started the horses for home.

T

Norman stood, waiting on the steps. The train ride had given him some time to think, but he knew he must wait to talk to the lawyer before anything was decided. Now the door was opened and a maid stood before him.

"Yes?"

Silently he handed her his card and after a quick glance

at it, she allowed him to enter the house. All was quiet as he stepped into the dark hall. The housekeeper was coming down the stairway and upon catching sight of him, gave an exclamation of delight. She had long been in the service of his grandmother, and when Norman used to come and visit as a child, she was the one who had made him feel at home.

"Master Norman, you have come at last!"

"Yes, Mrs. O'Connor, I'm here. I know I should have come sooner, but it is hard to get away from the ranch."

Mrs. O'Connor nodded. "Of course it is, but where is your wife?"

"Much to my regret, I had to leave her. You see, I only got the letter yesterday, and I can't stay long."

"Well, we can talk later. Mr. Athey is in the library, and I know he is anxious to talk to you."

Norman started toward the library door, but paused and asked, "Where's Orlena?"

"I'll see if I can't get her to come down to supper. She has hardly left her room since it happened. I don't know if her grief is real or only a show."

"Ah, Mr. Mavrich, I'm glad you have arrived safely." Mr. Athey stood up and held out his hand as Norman entered the library. "Although I regret that the necessity for your coming had to be these circumstances," he added.

Norman smiled. "I wish I could have come more often; however, ranch life doesn't exactly lend itself to absences very often."

"I understand."

The two gentlemen sat down in the great leather armchairs by the desk. Rows of shelves lined with books of every sort nearly filled two of the walls from floor to ceiling of the room while three large windows in heavy draperies served to lighten the room when the drapes were opened as they were now.

"What are the facts, Mr. Athey? Give me the basic thoughts and then we'll go on to fill in the details."

"Very well. It is really quite simple. Your grandmother left this house for your sister when she reaches twenty-one years of age. She also willed her a large sum of money to be held by you until she reaches that age. She had purchased years ago, a piece of land on which a mine was opened and which has been in operation for some time now. That land, with all the profit of the mining outfit, has been left to you. You, as I mentioned in my letter, I believe, are Orlena's only natural relative and therefore her only legal guardian until she reaches the age of twenty-one. This leaves you with the sole responsibility of deciding where she will live, what schools she shall attend and so forth. That is Mrs. Mavrich's entire last will and testament in a nutshell. Oh," he said, reaching for a file lying on the desk. "I almost forgot." Thumbing through the papers with which the file was crammed, he at last pulled out a sealed envelope and, holding it out to Norman, remarked quietly, "This was to be given to you in person."

Norman took the envelope and looked at the handwriting on the front. There was no doubt it was from his grandmother. The fancy curves and flourishes adorning his full name on the front was proof enough of that. Slowly he turned the thing over in his hand wondering what she had written.

Mr. Athey pulled out his watch and looked at the time; then he arose. "I'm afraid I will have to depart. I have another meeting which requires my presence, and I'm sure you must be tired after your trip. When would you like to meet again and finish this business?"

"Would this evening be convenient for you, Mr. Athey? I don't like to be away from the ranch longer than I have to, and—"

"I completely understand, Mr. Mavrich. This evening will be entirely satisfactory for me. Until this evening then," and with another handshake, the lawyer quietly departed leaving Norman alone in the library.

For several minutes he sat lost in thought, fingering the

envelope in his hands, pondering what he had heard. Then, as though he had been suddenly awakened, he stood, walked to a window and looked out, then turning, he too left the room.

It was an easy task for him to find Mrs. O'Connor and learn that Orlena was still in her room and that his own room was ready for him.

Mounting the stairs, he passed down the hall, the thickly carpeted floors giving back no sound of his footsteps. For a brief moment he paused beside his sister's room and listened. On hearing no sound within, he continued to his room, entered, and shut the door behind him.

Everything about him brought back memories. "Nothing has changed since I was here last," he murmured softly, running his hand over the ornately carved desk and fingering the rich fabric of the bedspread. He sighed. "How I dreaded coming here. Everything was so stiff and proper, Orlena was a—" he cleared his throat rather ruefully and left his sentence unfinished as he sat down by the open window watching the sun play across the floor and the cover of the bed. A little, warm puff of air blew in stirring his brown hair and causing the envelope still in his hand to sway.

"I almost forgot about this. I wonder what she has to say this time, " Norman mused, his brow a thoughtful frown while he broke the seal and pulled out the single sheet of delicate paper.

"To My Grandson Norman Mavrich," he read.

"When you read this, I will be in my grave and beyond the capability of trying to undo what I have done. I see now what I wouldn't see before, namely that I have, with my own hands and thoughtlessness spoiled your sister, Orlena. And now that I see what I have done, I am leaving her in your care. You tried to tell me, to show me the future, but I refused to listen. I have given Orlena everything she wanted if at all possible and always sided with her, often against you, in years past. I regret it deeply now and trust that you can forgive an old lady for her pride. I was so sure I knew how to raise a girl, though as you know, I never had but one son, your father. Well, I failed, miserably. Can you find it in your heart to try to undo the harm I have caused? Perhaps it is too late, but would you, for my sake, try? Your uncle raised you well after your parents' death. Hiram was never like me, and I wanted nothing to do with him after he bought that ranch. He was poor, except for what he earned by hard work, while I was rich. Yet my riches didn't bring happiness, not true happiness, to me or Orlena. Do what you can, Norman. For my sake, for the sake of your parents, and for the sake of your sister, I beg you, do your best to rescue Orlena from herself."

Triple Creek Ranch

T

CHAPTER 2

FIRST SKIRMISH

For a long time, Norman sat with the letter in his hand, staring into space. So, his grandmother had realized what she had done to Orlena, yet it was up to him and Jenelle to try and help her. He wondered how hard it would be. After all, he hadn't even seen his sister for over a year, and the last time he saw her was only for two days. What would she think of living on a ranch? A slight smile tugged at the corners of his mouth as he tried to picture Orlena milking cows or feeding chickens.

At last he roused and began to make himself presentable for table. He had no dinner jacket, only his best Sunday clothes which his wife had so carefully packed for him. These he donned, wishing she were here with him and wondering what she was doing.

These pleasant thoughts were interrupted by the dinner bell.

Again, as Norman passed down the hallway, he paused before his sister's door. Was she already at the table? Shrugging, he made his way down the broad stairway and into the dining room. There he found Mrs. O'Connor.

"I hope you had a nice rest, Norman," that good woman said. "You weren't wanting anything, were you?"

"Everything was quite comfortable, Mrs. O'Connor. Thank you. But," he raised an eyebrow and looked questioningly at the housekeeper, "is Orlena—?"

"That I do not know. She won't answer my knocks on the door. I even told her you had arrived, but as well I might have been talking to the china cabinet for all the reply I got."

Norman's brows drew together. Then, as one of the servants entered, he addressed her. "Go up to Miss Orlena's room, please, and say her brother awaits her in the dining room."

The maid dropped a curtsy and departed.

Softly drumming his fingers on the back of a chair, Norman waited. Would Orlena come? He rather doubted it. But he would wait a little while and see.

In a moment, the maid was back. "Please sir, Miss Orlena asks that you excuse her tonight."

Norman nodded, though he sighed to himself. "I don't think this will be very easy." Aloud he said, "Then, Mrs. O'Connor, you will join me for supper, won't you? I'm afraid it would be too lonely to eat by myself." His smile was bright and Mrs. O'Connor was happy to accept.

The meal, full of talk, of news and reminiscences, was a pleasant affair and helped dispel the feeling of oppression Norman always felt in his grandmother's stately mansion.

Hardly had the meal been concluded, when Mr. Athey was announced. Norman led the way to the library and shut the door behind them.

It was late when Mr. Athey departed, and Norman, after seeing the lawyer to the door, made his way through the darkened house to his room where a light had been left low. Closing the door and leaving the light dim, he slowly prepared for rest. His mind was busy with all he had heard and the decisions which must now be made. It felt like months ago that he had left his home. Surely it couldn't have been that morning!

At last, turning out the light, Norman dropped to his knees beside the bed. There, after spending much earnest time in prayer, he was filled with peace and, dropping wearily into bed, fell instantly to sleep.

"I did get a response out of Miss Orlena this morning, Norman." Mrs. O'Connor was bustling around the breakfast room preparing for the morning meal while the grandson of her late mistress looked on.

"Oh? And what did my sister have to say?"

"That she would be down to breakfast with you."

Norman's eyebrows raised in surprise. Perhaps things wouldn't be so hard after all. Could Orlena herself be wanting to change? Norman found himself, for the first time since he had arrived, looking forward to seeing his sister.

At that moment, the door opened, and Orlena entered. Though she was only twelve, Orlena Mavrich somehow managed to give the impression that she was at least sixteen by the way she carried herself and the fine, young lady styles she wore. At boarding school she, like the other young ladies, had been made to wear a uniform, but here in her grandmother's house, where she was allowed to do much as she liked, she dressed as she pleased. This morning her dress of rich black silk with the rows and rows of plaiting, ribbons and lace, as well as a slight train, gave her brother a start.

Who was this? Surely not his little sister! What could their grandmother have been thinking to let this child wear such ridiculous clothes? If the truth be known, Old Mrs. Mavrich would never have allowed such a get up, but upon her death, Orlena gave orders that she must have a proper mourning dress. None dared go against her wishes and thus the dress came to be.

Mrs. O'Connor watched Norman's face as he gazed in unconcealed astonishment. She saw his brows draw together and his mouth slowly settle into a frown. In the past this brother and sister had clashed nearly as often as they spoke, but always Mrs. Mavrich had been there to somehow smooth things over. At least, to smooth things for her beloved granddaughter. In vain Mrs. O'Connor had offered suggestions. Now, however, there was no one for Orlena to fly to if her will was crossed in any way, and the good housekeeper could only wait, wondering what would happen. She didn't have long to wait, for Orlena broke the silence.

"So, Norman, you have decided to come for a visit after Grandmother is dead." She gave a sniff and dabbed at her eyes with a fine, lace-trimmed handkerchief.

Swallowing back a retort he knew he would regret, Norman forced himself to smile and say calmly, "I wish I could have come at a more pleasant time, but ranch life wasn't made for frequent absences."

Orlena continued with a slight pout on her pretty face as she was seated at the table, "I suppose you will have to rush off as usual to that ridiculous ranch tomorrow. Or do you have to go today?" Without giving her brother a chance to so much as agree or disagree, she went on. "You never do stay long. I sometimes think you must not like me. I don't see what you find to interest you way out in the middle of nowhere. Now, if you would only move to the city, I'm sure you would soon become a brother I could be proud of showing to my friends. Why don't you stay in town, Norman?"

"You forget I'm married, Orlena." The reply was slightly cold, although Norman was striving to keep his temper under control.

"Oh well, of course you can send for your wife. I think it is about time I met my sister again. Why didn't you bring her with you? Is she afraid of the city? I have heard all country girls are." How fast Orlena's tongue could fly.

Mrs. O'Connor, watching the brother and sister, could see the growing set of Norman's face and caught a glimpse of the flash in his eyes which he tried to keep directed towards his plate. As for Orlena, her pert mouth and the haughty toss of her head made the housekeeper predict to herself that Orlena was setting herself up for a clash of arms with her brother. She knew who would win in the end, for Norman had the upper hand this time in that he was now Orlena's guardian, but who would triumph in this first skirmish was yet to be seen.

At last Norman broke in to his sister's chatter. "Orlena, suppose you eat and let me talk for a little while, seeing that I have finished and you have scarcely begun."

A sniff came from across the table. "How can I eat when I miss Grandmother," whimpered Orlena. "You don't know what it is like to be left all alone at the mercy of servants who think they can do what they please now. I have been perfectly miserable. There was no one to talk to and—" another sniff ended the complaint.

"I am very sorry for the loss of Grandmother," began Norman, trying to speak kindly.

"And I didn't think you would ever come," whined the spoiled child across from him. "Why do you have to go back to that horrid, old ranch and—"

"Orlena! Be quiet." The stern voice startled her into silence, but only for a moment.

"Oh, how can you talk to me that way?" she wailed. "You don't love me. No one does!" and with her handkerchief to her eyes she rushed out of the room slamming the door behind her.

Not until the distant slam of Orlena's door was also heard, did Norman move. Then, after a deep sigh, he began to drum his fingers on the table, a habit he had when perplexed. Looking over at Mrs. O'Connor, he gave a slight smile. "That didn't go so well. What do I do now?"

Mrs. O'Connor wisely kept silent, knowing that no word of hers would be needed and Norman didn't expect an answer.

Rising from the table, he slowly moved from the room with head bowed. Had he spoken in haste things which he should repent of? Going back over the few words he did speak, Norman didn't think so. How was he to talk to Orlena? It must be done, and the sooner things were clear between them, the better it would be for both brother and sister. Before going to Orlena's room, Norman slipped into his own and again spent some time in prayer.

Soon after, Norman knocked gently on his sister's door.

"Who is it?" crossly demanded Orlena.

"It is me, please open the door, Sis."

"Go away, I don't want to talk to you!"

"But we need to talk. Come on, Orlena," was the patient reply, "either let me in or go with me to another room were we can talk alone."

For a long minute all was still. Norman wasn't at all sure if Orlena would open the door or not.

"What if I don't want to talk to you?" The question, though still somewhat testy, held an element of wonder in it, as though Orlena really wanted to know if her brother would let her have her own way or not.

"Then I'm sorry, for I must talk with you." There was something in Norman's voice which seemed to compel compliance though it was neither stern nor harsh.

Slowly the door opened and Orlena appeared with a pout.

"Do you want to talk here or somewhere else?" Norman asked gently.

Orlena shrugged, then held open the door into her little sitting room.

It was only after they were both sitting, Orlena curled up in a chair like a little kitten ready to spit and scratch if its fur was rubbed the wrong way, and her brother in a chair opposite, that Norman began.

"I've been going over affairs with Grandmother's lawyer," he began slowly, "and things are going to change, drastically I'm afraid. For one, this house is going to be closed. There is no need to keep it open and pay for the help needed to run it when none of us will be here. Mr. Athey is going to see if he can find a family to rent it until such a time as we might want it again." Pausing a moment to look at his sister, Norman was surprised to find her seemingly indifferent to this news. Encouraged by this he continued, waiting and bracing himself, however, for the explosion he felt sure would come sometime, though uncertain which news would be the match to light it.

"You will be leaving with me, in two days, for the ranch—"

Orlena bounced from her chair, eyes flashing. The match had been lit.

CHAPTER 3

HOME

"I'll do nothing of the kind!" she fairly shouted. "I wouldn't go to that old place if you paid me all the gold in China!"

Norman's quiet voice was a marked contrast to Orlena's angry one as he replied, "Good, because no one is going to pay you anything. Just the same, you are coming to live with Jenelle and me on the ranch."

"Who says so?"

"I do."

Orlena glared at her brother. "I won't go. You can't make me. I'm going to Madam Viscount's Seminary."

"Orlena, I'm your legal guardian and you *are* coming to the ranch."

Then Orlena gave way to a tantrum just as she used to when, as a five-year-old, her will had been thwarted. She screamed and cried, stomping her feet and throwing whatever she could lay her hands on in her anger until Norman, grasping her shoulders, pushed her into her chair and held her there.

"Orlena, that is enough!" Never had Norman's voice been that stern.

The screaming stopped, but Orlena continued to cry and struggle. "I didn't get a sister, I got a wildcat," muttered Norman between tightly clenched teeth. His temper was roused and it was all he could do to keep from shaking the girl before him. All he could do was silently pray for help, for he had no idea what to do. Had it been a brother instead of a sister, Norman would undoubtedly have administered a severe chastisement.

It was several minutes before Orlena quieted down enough for her brother to draw up a chair before hers. "I know you don't want to go with me," he began slowly, searching for the right words, "but I'm afraid you have no choice. Jenelle is waiting for you, and I think, if you are willing to give it a chance, you will learn in time to like it."

A glare was the only reply he got.

"I can't leave the ranch, I have too many responsibilities, and I can't leave you by yourself."

"Why not?" she demanded.

Norman's eyebrows rose. "I think you just showed a good display of why not. If you can't control yourself from exhibitions of that sort when something doesn't suit your fancy, then you are not old enough to stay by yourself anywhere."

"What about school?" The question was petulant.

"That hasn't been decided yet."

"Well, I'll have you understand one thing here and now, Norman Mavrich," Orlena's voice became that of a haughty princess, "I am going to attend Madam Viscount's Seminary as I did last year. Nothing you can say or do will prevent me."

Wisely, Norman held his tongue and refrained from replying. He hoped desperately that she would forget about that place before school started again, but one thing he knew for certain, she was not going back to Madam Viscount's Seminary!

Finding no reply coming from her brother, and assuming that he had surrendered to her in regards to school, she yielded to her curiosity and asked, "What else is going to change?"

"Well," he longed to say, 'your clothes', but wasn't sure if it would be wise yet, so he merely said, "Those are all the major changes. We will be packing a few trunks to ship out to the ranch, but we don't have room for everything. Mr. Athey, along with Mrs. O'Connor, will take care of the details of the house. I think we had better stir ourselves so that the necessary packing can be done before we have to leave." Norman rose from his seat as he talked, then, looking down at his sister, he added gently, "I hope you will enjoy the ranch, Orlena. You and I haven't spent much time together and don't know each other all that well; perhaps that is mostly my fault for not coming to visit much. Now we have a chance to fix that and I hope we make the most of it." With those last few words, he quietly withdrew from the room, leaving his sister silent.

How Norman ever lived through the rest of that day and the following one was never quite clear in his own mind. He knew he was constantly busy helping pack, answering hundreds of questions, trying to keep his temper with Orlena and a multitude of other things, but at last he was seated beside his sister as the train pulled away from the station. They were heading home.

The thought of seeing Jenelle again and getting away from the noise and bustle of the city kept Norman quiet and, though he kept a careful watch of his sister's comforts, his mind was preoccupied. What would Orlena think of the ranch? What would Jenelle think of Orlena? Perhaps that was a more important question. Norman knew his sweet wife was longing to be a sister and friend to Orlena, but if she knew what she was really like— He never let himself finish the sentence, partly because he had no idea what he would do if Jenelle decided that Orlena was beyond help, and partly out of a longing that Orlena had only been putting on an act when he used to visit. That last was a vain hope, and deep in his heart he knew it was, yet how anyone could be so selfish and stuck-up was beyond him.

Sitting beside her quiet brother in a traveling suit of the latest style, Orlena pouted. She had done nothing else it seemed since she had first been told she must go live on a ranch. If she had to go, she would at least make it very clear to everyone that she did not like it. Since Norman was either ignoring her on purpose or hadn't noticed her disgust, she fell to wondering what her new, well, she wouldn't call it home, was like. She would only be staying there for a few months before going back to her boarding school. What would it be like living in the country that she saw only through train car windows?

With a shriek of its whistle and a hiss of its brakes, the train pulled to a stop at the little station where Jenelle Mavrich stood waiting. Eagerly she watched the few passengers alight. As Norman swung himself off and then turned to assist his sister down, Jenelle hurried over to them.

"Norman!"

"Darling!" And Jenelle found herself once more in her husband's arms while he bent and kissed her. For a moment neither of them remembered the silent, aloof sister standing in disgust as she looked at her surroundings.

At last Jenelle freed herself with a little laugh and turned to the figure in black. "You must be Orlena. Welcome to Rough Rock. I'm Jenelle." And she kissed her new sister with warmth. "You don't know how delighted I have been knowing that you were coming. Norman, can you get the bags? I'll take Orlena to the wagon." Linking her arm through Orlena's, Jenelle led the way over to the wagon talking in that sweet, pleasant way of hers though not a word had Orlena vouchsafed in answer to even her greeting.

It was only a matter of a few minutes before Norman joined them with the bags which he stowed in the back of the wagon. After he helped his wife and sister onto the wagon seat, he picked up the reins, clicked to the horses and they were off for the Triple Creek Ranch.

Sitting silent and half afraid, Orlena grasped the side of the seat until her knuckles turned white. She had never ridden on a wagon like this before. It swayed and bumped over the rutted road. And the dust! It fairly seemed to smother her though neither Norman nor Jenelle appeared to notice it at all.

"Orlena," Norman said at last, looking over Jenelle's head to his sister. "You can see the ranch when we reach the top of this hill. It will only be a few moments before we reach home."

Turning her lip up in disgust at the word "home," Orlena nevertheless looked out at the wide sprawling ranch buildings, pastures and fields as they stretched before her and was, to her annoyance, impressed at the vastness of it all. She had never dreamed her brother owned so much. When she was at school it would be something to tell her classmates, something she could boast about: how large her brother's ranch out west was. But now she was going to have to live here!

The wagon pulled to a stop before a good sized house. It wasn't a typical ranch style house for it had been built as a farm house long before Norman's great-uncle Hiram had begun his ranch. Two stories high, and nearly surrounded by shade trees, the house looked pleasant and inviting to weary travelers. At least it did to Norman. His sister gave it a scornful look and turned up her pert nose.

"Welcome home, Orlena," Jenelle smiled brightly. "I'm sure you must be tired from your trip, so let me show you to your room. Your trunks arrived yesterday, and I had Hearter take them right up. I didn't have time to unpack for you, but I thought you might enjoy doing that later." As Jenelle spoke, she led the way into the cool front room and up the stairs to a small but cozy and quite comfortable room. It was a corner one with windows on two sides looking out over the barn yard on the one side and a large field on the other.

Still silent, Orlena walked about her new room, noticed the light curtains tied back with bits of pink ribbon, the bed with its patchwork quilt and the rag rug beside it, noticed also the small closet and toilet stand in one corner and the chair and writing table in another. Everything had been made as dainty and pretty, as clean and neat as her sister-in-law's hands could make things. Yet, in her eyes, when compared to the splendor of what she had left only that morning, Orlena thought she might as well have been sent to sleep in the barn!

She didn't say these things, only thought them, but her expressive face betrayed somewhat of her inner feelings. Jenelle didn't speak either but watched this young girl with feelings of deepest pity and love.

Coming in with Orlena's bags, Norman set them down and said, turning to his wife, "I'm hungry, what is smelling so good downstairs?"

Jenelle laughed, "Your supper. Mrs. Carmond kindly lent me Flo for the day to get ready for you both. She made supper so that I might meet you at the station. But, Dear, you should freshen up a bit before we eat."

"That does sound pleasant. Orlena, we'll leave you to do the same."

"If you need anything, just call me," Jenelle added gently before shutting the door after them.

Alone in their own room on the other side of the house, Jenelle looked thoughtful. "Norman," she began at last.

"Hmm," came the somewhat distracted response.

"Orlena seems very quiet. I don't think she has said more than two words since your arrival on the train."

Vigorous splashes of water from the washstand, where Norman was busy washing the dust of travel off his face, prevented any reply.

Jenelle continued, "Does Orlena talk much or is she always quiet?"

Turning abruptly, unmindful of the water running down his face and dripping onto the floor, Norman stared at his wife. "Talk?" he gasped. "Does she talk? She can talk faster than I can rope a calf! And once she starts, she doesn't stop!" Then, suddenly realizing the mess he was making, he grabbed a towel and buried his face in it.

"I predict," he added a moment later, looking at his wife in the mirror as she perched schoolgirl fashion on the bed and leaned against the post, "that in a few days you'll be wishing she would stop talking so you can think."

Jenelle only smiled.

Dropping the hairbrush he had been using, Norman suddenly stepped across the room, put a finger under Jenelle's chin and lifted her face up to look deep into her blue eyes which sparkled with life, joy and love. "Sweetheart," he whispered tenderly, "I love you."

Triple Creek Ranch

T

CHAPTER 4

MISTRESS OF TRIPLE CREEK

The clock on the mantle ticked loudly and Norman drummed his fingers on his chair. Supper was ready and waiting, and he was hungry. He would have liked to eat quickly and go out to talk with Hardrich, his foreman, about the ranch, but Orlena had yet to make an appearance. Where was she?

"I'm going to go see what is keeping her, Norman," Jenelle came into the dining room from the kitchen.

Mounting the stairs lightly, Jenelle wondered if her new sister had fallen asleep, worn out by the trip, or if she was crying for homesickness. "The poor dear," she thought as she approached Orlena's door. "Orlena," she called gently as she knocked softly.

"Come in," was the calm and completely unexpected answer.

In amazement, Jenelle opened the door to behold Orlena with hair loose, seated in the chair near the east window. She didn't appear to be homesick or even extra tired. She looked simply bored.

"Yes?"

"Supper is ready and waiting. Aren't you going to come join us?"

Speaking in the haughty fashion she used for her grandmother's servants, this young, spoiled girl replied, "I

wish my supper served to me here. I don't want to go down."
She shrugged.

"Are you feeling all right?" Jenelle was puzzled by this
state of things.

"I am just fine. I only wish my supper served in my
room. And send the girl up to unpack my trunks. I wish to
supervise while it is done. That will be all," she added as
Jenelle opened her mouth as though to say something.

Feeling herself dismissed, Mrs. Norman Mavrich
withdrew and shut the door. For the first time in her life she
had been ordered away with instructions of what she must
do, and all by a mere child. Always one to find the humorous
side of things, by the time she reached the stairs, she couldn't
hold back her laughter.

On reaching the dining room she sank onto a chair
putting her hands over her mouth to try and suppress her
merriment.

"Jenelle, what is it? Is she coming down? Darling,
you're laughing." Norman exclaimed, striding across the
room to stand in front of her. "What is going on?" He folded
his arms and stood waiting.

"Oh, I suppose I really shouldn't laugh, but it was all so
comical and not in the least what I was expecting." And she
burst into fresh giggles.

Her husband tried to look annoyed, but couldn't keep
back a grin. His wife's amusement was contagious. "Then do
share it, Darling, for really I am quite famished. I was too
busy to eat in the city before we left and I haven't had a bite
since."

As he figured, Jenelle's sympathies were instantly
aroused, and she sprang up. "Oh you poor thing! Just sit
down and I'll have Flo bring it right out. It is a shame to have
made you wait. And I know you want to go talk with
Hardrich."

"What about Orlena?" Norman wanted to know as the
steaming dishes were brought out.

"She asked that her supper be served to her room since

she didn't want to come down this evening."

"No."

Jenelle looked up somewhat startled. "What?"

"Unless she is sick, Orlena will eat her meals with us here in the dining room." Norman's voice was firm and full of decision. "I don't want to be harsh, but if we give in to her every whim now—" he looked at his wife for support.

She smiled. "Of course. I can see no reason why Orlena must have her meal served in her room except that she is used to being catered to."

Norman placed his napkin on the table and half rose, "I'll go tell her."

"No, Dear," Jenelle put in sweetly, "you eat. I'll tell her. You are much too tired to try dealing with your sister tonight. I'll manage." And before Norman could protest, she had slipped from the room.

Though still somewhat amused by Orlena's earlier orders, Jenelle had a feeling that Miss Orlena wouldn't be amused by her refusal to follow them. What would Orlena do? Would she submit and come down to eat in the dining room or would she stay in her room? What if she refused to leave her room tomorrow unless her wishes were granted? For the first time since Norman had told her of old Mrs. Mavrich's passing, Jenelle began to wonder how they would manage with this young household tyrant. She was thankful she had refrained from mentioning to Norman all Orlena's words.

Opening the door in answer to the command, Jenelle refrained from dropping a curtsy at the look of aloof superiority on Orlena's countenance. Before she had time to say anything, the new member of the Triple Creek Ranch burst forth.

"Where is my supper? It has taken long enough to have gone half way to China by now. And where is the girl to unpack my trunks? Why didn't you send her up?"

Jenelle quietly closed the door before replying. "If you wish to eat, your place is waiting for you in the dining room.

Norman had to eat quickly so that he could have a talk with our foreman. As for the 'girl,' she is only here for a little while longer and I'm afraid doesn't have time to unpack for you. If you would like, you and I can do it together tomorrow."

Then Jenelle was treated to a flash of eyes and a blaze of cheeks which rivaled a fireworks display on the Fourth of July. Orlena was furious. Not only had her wishes been tossed aside by this "mere sister-in-law," but her brother apparently didn't care about her now that he was back on his ranch. For a moment, Orlena remained seated then rising, she found her voice. "I won't go down! Bring my supper to me at once!" Orlena stamped her foot.

Jenelle merely shook her head with a soft smile.

"Do you realize who I am?" stormed the angry child with hands on her hips and glaring eyes. Then, without giving Jenelle time to answer had she wanted to, the haughty princess continued, "I am Orlena Mavrich, the only granddaughter and sole heir of the late Mrs. Marshall Mavrich of Blank City and as such I demand you respect my wishes!"

Long before this was over, Jenelle earnestly hoped her husband had finished his meal and gone out to speak to the foreman. He was already tired and didn't need to deal with his sister right now.

When Orlena had finished, Jenelle sat down on the edge of the bed and began to speak quietly yet with a half amused, half determined voice. "Suppose you and I come to an understanding right now, Orlena. You are, as you say, the only granddaughter of the late Mrs. Marshall Mavrich. But it is also true that I am the wife of Norman Mavrich, who is your legal guardian, and the only grandson of the same Mrs. Marshall Mavrich and as such am the mistress of this house. When I tell you that unless you are sick, no meals will be served to your room, that is exactly what I mean. Now, should you choose to come down and eat, I would be most happy to have you. Otherwise, you can wait until breakfast. It is up to you." Jenelle remained where she was sitting and watched her new young sister.

Never had Orlena had anyone speak to her in that manner. Norman would have become stern, Grandmother would have coaxed and pleaded, the servants would have trembled, and even the instructors of Madam Viscount's Seminary would have given in, but here was this woman who showed none of the usual signs. For once in her life, Orlena was speechless.

Jenelle took advantage of this moment and added, rising and stepping to the door, "If you wish to eat with me, I will be downstairs. Or," she added as a second thought, "you may eat in the kitchen if you prefer." And before Orlena could find her tongue, Mrs. Norman Mavrich had slipped from the room and disappeared.

Downstairs, she found that Norman had eaten in haste and left the house. Feeling relieved, she sank into a chair and began slowly to eat her meal. This wouldn't be as easy as she had expected. Her husband had been right when he said his little sister was a terror. What were they going to do with her? Suppose she wouldn't come down to eat? Was she going to stay up in her room by herself? Sighing, Jenelle shook her head and began talking to herself, a habit she had when working through problems. "Obviously she can't stay in that room for too long. She'll have to eat, so she must come down. But what will Norman do? Jenelle Mavrich, stop worrying. This is only the first evening; the poor girl is probably so overcome by the newness of things and the sudden move and changes that she doesn't really know what she wants."

Here her low murmurings were interrupted. "Mrs. Mavrich?"

Jenelle turned. Flo Carmond stood in the doorway.

"My father is here to take me home if you don't need me any longer."

"No, I can handle the rest by myself. Thank you so much, Flo. You were a tremendous help. And be sure you tell your mother how much I appreciate her lending you to me." Jenelle's smile was bright as she watched the sturdy young girl hurry out to swing up behind her father on his horse and ride off across the fields towards the Carmond ranch.

When Norman came in from the barn later that evening, as the sun was beginning to sink in the horizon, he found his wife seated with her sewing in the cool front room of the house. Orlena was no where to be seen. "Where's Orlena?"

Jenelle looked up. "Still in her room I presume."

"Did she come down to supper?"

Jenelle turned her eyes back to her sewing and shook her head. "Did you have a talk with Hardrich?" she asked, trying to change the subject.

Norman sat down in an easy chair across from his wife. "Yes, and it looks like he has done a good job of things. What did my sister say when you told her her supper would not be served to her room?"

"Many things," replied Jenelle evasively.

For a moment the rancher remained silent watching Jenelle's fingers as they sewed tiny stitches in a colorful quilt. Then he spoke. "Aren't you going to tell me what she said?"

Jenelle glanced up. "You are too tired to be bothered with your sister tonight. No," she hastened to add as she saw Norman open his mouth to speak while his eyebrows drew together, "there is no need for you to try to come to my defense. I left her speechless when I came away and I haven't heard anything from her since."

Still Norman continued to frown. "If she has been impertinent to you—"

"Now Norman," Jenelle interrupted him, and, laying aside her sewing, went and sat on the arm of his chair. "Orlena is young. There have been a lot of changes in her life in the last few weeks; she lost her grandmother with whom she spent nearly all of her life, she had to leave the city and come out to the middle of nowhere to live with a brother she hardly knows and his wife who is practically a complete stranger to her. She is tired and worn out. Give her a little time to adjust before you let yourself get worked up about her." She kissed him and was pulled onto his knee.

That first night at the Triple Creek Ranch was, to Orlena, a night never to be forgotten. She had heard her brother and sister-in-law come up the stairs after the sun had almost disappeared leaving her room dusky. She hadn't lit the lamp for the gloom suited her mood better. Hearing soft footsteps approaching her door, Orlena stiffened in her chair. Who was it and what did they want? A gentle knock sounded. Then, when she didn't respond, Jenelle's voice speaking quietly came through the closed door.

"Good-night, Orlena. Sleep well."

Orlena didn't reply and the footsteps turned and were soon gone.

Then indeed did this young girl from the city feel alone. Never in all her eleven years of life had she known such stillness. No streetcars going past, no voices down on the sidewalks, no late carriages leaving for or returning from a party, concert or social event. Here all was still and quiet, too quiet, she thought, almost holding her breath in the unfamiliar and, to her, fearful hush which had descended on everything. Not a sound could she hear besides the beating of her heart.

Suddenly, with trembling fingers, Orlena reached out and lit the lamp. Its bright glow helped to diminish the feelings of terror which had swept over her as Jenelle's footsteps had died away. This place, she realized with almost a start, this silent, small place was to be her home. Here she must live day after day with her brother and his wife, at least until school started. Eagerly she began trying to count the days left before the new term opened, but the fatigues of the day as well as her passionate outburst had worn down her strength and, after a moment of trying, she gave it up.

Rising slowly, she soon arrayed herself for bed and in disgust, lay down on the neatly made bed and pulled the quilt over herself. She turned down the light but didn't dare put it out completely. She didn't know what unknown terrors the night held for her and she didn't care to face them in the dark in this unfamiliar place.

CHAPTER 5

ENCOUNTERS

"Jenelle," Norman asked as the two of them seated themselves at the breakfast table, "isn't my sister going to come down?"

Laughing softly, Jenelle poured her husband his coffee before replying. "Darling, you forget that Orlena is a city girl. They don't eat breakfast at this unearthly hour. Besides, when I looked in at her, she was sound asleep. The poor child is tired. Let her sleep. I'm sure she'll be down later."

Though Norman frowned a little, he could see the wisdom in Jenelle's words and nodded his head.

Jenelle had been right, never had Orlena risen much less breakfasted at such an early hour in her life. When she did awake, the sun was already several hours high. At first she didn't know where she was and lay staring about her in bewilderment. Then it all came flooding back to her and she sat up. She was at the ranch, her brother's ranch! It was at that time that she remembered her clothes were still packed in her trunk. In great disgust she unlocked and raised the lid. After several minutes of rummaging around, she finally pulled from its depths the black, silk dress in which Norman had first seen her. Shaking out the folds, she held it up to her and looked into the small mirror on the wall.

"If I wear this, that rude sister-in-law of mine will know that I'm not to be trifled with. And perhaps it will show my brother that I'm not a child to be ordered around."

It took Orlena longer than usual to dress, for she could not just press a button and summon a maid to assist her in buttoning up the thirty-seven buttons which adorned her mourning costume. At last she was ready and, feeling the gnawing pangs of hunger, she ventured forth from her room.

Though she wouldn't have admitted it to anyone, Orlena was curious, as most younger ones are, and older ones too, when they are in a new place. Moving slowly about, she quietly peered into rooms and looked about before moving down the stairs.

Jenelle was busy churning when Orlena finally swept her way into the kitchen after wandering about the lower regions of the house. Jenelle had heard her come down and decided to let her have some time to explore, knowing that eventually she would end up in the kitchen if she was as hungry as Jenelle imagined her to be.

"Good morning, Orlena," Jenelle greeted the young girl with a smile, trying not to give a start at the sight of the dress. "I hope you slept well. Norman is already at work in the fields. I imagine you are hungry. Would you prefer to eat in here or in the dining room?"

"Only servants eat in the kitchen," and Orlena tossed her head disdainfully.

"In that case, suppose you have a seat in the dining room and I'll soon bring your breakfast to you, unless you would like to stay and watch. The butter has just come and it will only take me a few minutes to work it." Jenelle had spoken as she would have to anyone, but Orlena rolled her eyes and with a sniff, swept out of the kitchen.

"If she keeps on sweeping about in that dress," Jenelle murmured to herself as she swiftly set to work salting and patting the butter into balls, "I won't have to sweep the house."

Only a few minutes later, Jenelle carried in and set before her young guest a plate of bread and butter, a glass of fresh milk and an egg in an egg cup.

"Where is my coffee?" demanded the girl.

Jenelle raised her eyebrows in surprise. "Coffee?" she repeated. "Only Norman and the hands drink coffee."

"I drink it," Orlena stated emphatically, "milk is for babies."

Jenelle looked completely unconcerned as she shrugged, removing the offending glass. "Very well, if you don't want any fresh milk, I'll get you a glass of water."

"Bring coffee," Orlena ordered as her sister-in-law disappeared into the kitchen.

To this, however, Jenelle made no reply, gave no indication by look or manner that she had even heard the demand and, returning moments later with a glass of water, set it gently down beside Orlena's plate.

Before Orlena could do more than open her mouth, Jenelle spoke hurriedly. "I must leave you to your breakfast, Orlena, and attend to my bread at once or it will run over. When that is out of the way, I will be free to show you about the ranch, if you wish." And then she vanished, quietly, quickly, without rustle of silk or petticoat, leaving a very astonished girl behind her.

For one long minute Orlena sat in silence, once again left speechless by the mistress of the ranch. Then, finding the pangs of hunger quite demanding, she began to eat. Since she had eaten no supper the night before, and had only a little to eat on the train, she made a hearty breakfast in spite of not having coffee to drink.

When at last, her hunger satisfied, she rose from the table, a feeling of independence came over her. She didn't need anyone to show her around like she was some ignorant, backward child; she could and would go by herself. Wasn't she used to the city? Out here in the middle of nowhere there weren't even streetcars to watch out for. She would simply take a stroll around the ranch and see if she could by some far stretch of the imagination discover a hint of why Norman would not leave this miserable place and move to the city.

So, leaving her dirty dishes on the table, Orlena

ventured outside, forgetting all about the dress she was wearing with its long train and ruffles and plaiting and lace. She was going to explore the Triple Creek Ranch herself.

Now, if Orlena had been raised on a ranch or even on a farm, she would have fared much better than she and her dress did, for this was not the city she was used to with its sidewalks and stores, its policemen and newsboys, its fashionably dressed ladies and their faultlessly attired escorts; where the only animals were horses hitched to carriages and an occasional pet dog on a leash; with the only feathered fowls being the pigeons and sparrows and now and then some brave little song bird venturing forth from the shelter of its nest in search of a crumb for its young. This young, spoiled child of wealth realized only too late the folly of her decision.

Orlena's first stop was the barn which she had seen from her window. Striving to hold her dress off the dusty ground, she arrived in the doorway and peered in. All was quiet, for Norman and the hired hands were all hard at work in the fields, as were the horses. Slowly the brown haired newcomer stepped into the shadowy aisle. It was cooler there in the shade than out in the sun, she realized. Suddenly a noise startled her and she whirled around, not noticing her dress catching on a loose nail in the door.

"Meow."

Orlena gasped. There before her was a sleek, calico cat. With another meow, the cat came towards her and rubbed against the silky folds of the "latest style" black mourning dress!

"Oh, get away you . . . you creature!" Orlena fumed, lifting her skirts and trying to move away. The train of her dress was stuck on the nail. "Go away you horrid thing!" She ventured a little kick and the cat, feeling its reception was cold, stalked on with its tail twitching in supreme indignation. Orlena, watching the departing animal, snorted in disgust and gave an impatient jerk to her skirt.

Ri-i-p! The skirt was free. "Well, Norman will just have

to send it back to the dressmakers to fix it," she thought, trying to see how bad the tear was, but in the dim light it was difficult.

With a scowl she dropped her dress and moved on down the aisle of the barn. It never occurred to her to look down at her feet or to think of what the train of her dress would be sweeping up. The rest of the barn was empty of life, for the horses were out with the men or in the corrals, as were the few milk cows.

Blinking in the bright sun as she stepped from the door on the opposite side of the barn, Orlena paused. To her left she saw several high, fenced corrals while on the right and straight before her she saw fields and hills. Being out in the hot, summer sun with her heavy, black dress, she didn't feel like doing much walking, so she chose to visit the corrals.

Approaching the first one, she saw several horses. Swiftly pulling out her lace trimmed handkerchief she pressed it against her nose.

"How disgusting. It smells," she grumbled. "I wish school started today!" She looked away across the hot fields where not a tree grew.

A soft nicker caused her to turn her head. One of the horses, evidently wondering why this person was here, had come over to investigate. Thrusting its nose over the fence, it began to lip Orlena's hair and blow in her face.

"Oh, you vile beast!" she exclaimed, starting back. "I'll teach you to mind your manners with me!" And picking up a stick which lay conveniently nearby, she struck at the horse's head. She missed, and the startled animal let out a whinny and reared, pawing at the fence with its front hooves.

A little scared, but mostly angry that a mere horse would dare resist her, she raised the stick again, shouting, "I'll make you obey, you stupid animal!"

As the irate girl was about to strike once more, someone grasped her arm and the stick was jerked from her hand.

"We don't strike horses like that on the Triple Creek!" a

stern voice commanded.

Orlena turned around to see a stranger eyeing her from under his cowboy hat as he stood, arms crossed and booted feet planted firmly.

Instantly the girl's anger turned from the horse to this stranger. "Who do you think you are that you can order me around?" she haughtily demanded.

The man had turned from her to the horse and was attempting to calm it. "Easy girl. No one's goin' to hurt you." Without so much as turning his head, he replied to Orlena, "I'm Lloyd Hearter. I work here."

Orlena stamped her foot, planted her hands on her hips and stormed, "You look at me when I speak to you. Do you even know who I am?"

"Yep," the young hand replied and again kept his eyes on the horse who was trotting around the corral in a nervous manner.

"Then look at me! I'll have Norman fire you if you don't follow my orders."

Then the man slowly turned and looked at the spoiled girl before him. In a calm but deliberate way he spoke, "I follow Mr. Mavrich's orders and Mrs. Mavrich's, but no one ever told me to follow the orders of anyone else unless it was Hardrich. Now," he continued, "never strike the animals again!" Then turning, he simply walked back towards the barn with an easy stride, leaving Orlena to fume and fuss behind him.

"I'll tell Norman," she threatened the cowboy's back. "I'll make him fire you. You can't give me orders. I give orders!" And she stamped her foot again.

Lloyd gave no heed to her words and disappeared into the barn.

Fuming with indignation, Orlena swept on past the corrals. "Ordering me around like that! I'll speak to Norman first thing and make him fire that impudent servant." How she would make her brother do anything if he didn't want to never crossed her mind. She hadn't lived long enough with folks who couldn't be bent to her way by some means or another to know that it could prove a very difficult task.

The sun was blazing down, making this city girl uncomfortably warm in her yards and yards of heavy black silk. Pausing to look about her, Orlena discovered that she was on the top of a small hill. Behind her she could see the house, barn and a few of the other buildings. Before her, in the valley, stood some trees, the shade of which looked invitingly cool.

"I don't want to go back to the house yet," she mused. "I will just go on down to those trees." This decided, down the hill she went, her dress catching on rocks and brambles as she descended, tearing and snagging the lace, ruffles and plaitings. With a satisfied smile, Orlena jerked her dress. "Now Norman will see that I don't belong out in the middle of no where and will have to send me back to the city," she thought in triumph. It never occurred to her that, though her dress might not be proper for ranch life, there were other clothes to wear.

Entering the shade of the trees, Orlena discovered a small creek which rippled and gurgled over stones in a manner most soothing and satisfying even to this city bred child. Seating herself on a rock, she sat in complete silence listening to the music of the creek and longing, yet not daring, to take off her heavy shoes and stockings and dip her feet in the cool, refreshing stream. She knew it was cool, for she touched it with her hands, letting them stay in the water, enjoying the new sensation of the small current pushing them, moving them, swirling around them when they remained where they were.

It was all so new and charming that Orlena lost track of the time and of where she was. All reality vanished and memories of the pleasures of her former life claimed her mind, leaving her sitting dazed and dreaming.

CHAPTER 6

THE SMELL OF TROUBLE

"There you are, Lloyd," one of the hands greeted the returning young man.

"What took you so long?" questioned another.

"I met the newest member of the ranch."

"What's she like?"

"Just like Mavrich said, she's a wildcat. She said she was going to have the boss fire me." This was spoken with great apparent amusement.

"Who said I was going to fire you?" Norman had just ridden up and caught the last few words.

Lloyd glanced up. "Your sister."

Norman frowned but Lloyd only grinned.

"Guess you'll have to, Boss."

The others were chuckling as though the whole thing was a joke, so Mr. Mavrich, swallowing his anger, replied, "You're fired, Hearter!"

Hearing the ringing of a bell made Orlena start suddenly and look up. No longer was she in the city with her grandmother, she was out on a ranch with her brother and his wife. Her life had changed and not for the better, she grumbled. The light in the trees looked different. She stood up. It was late. Then she remembered, she must hurry back to the house and make Norman fire that insolent man!

Starting back through the trees, she suddenly saw something move out of the corner of her eye. Peering more closely at it, she saw a small black and white animal. "Another one of those cats," she snorted in disgust. "I'll teach this one to leave me alone." Searching about she soon discovered a few small rocks. Picking one up, she threw it in the direction of the animal.

"Go away!" she scolded. The rock didn't come close at all to it and Orlena threw another one. This one landed right next to the black and white creature and when the following rock hit it, the animal raised its tail.

Norman had finished brushing his horse when Jenelle came into the barn. He looked up and greeted her with a kiss.

"How was your day?" he asked.

"Quiet," Jenelle replied stooping to pick up a small kitten that was attempting to climb her skirt. "Orlena has been out since she ate breakfast. She—"

But she got no farther, for at that moment a sudden, terrified scream filled the air!

In a flash, Norman was out of the barn glancing about. The scream came again and he rushed towards the hill followed by his wife, while the foreman and the hired hands poured from the bunkhouse. At the top of the hill Norman halted suddenly and ordered firmly, "Orlena, stop right there."

"A skunk," Jenelle half moaned before calling a few of the hands to go fetch some jars of tomatoes. "Norman, you take her out to the pump behind the barn. I'll fetch some clean clothes and more tomatoes and then I'll take over."

Norman nodded, turning his head away as he beckoned his sister. The smell was almost nauseating.

Thirty minutes later, Jenelle and Orlena made their way to the dining room where supper was waiting. The smell of the skunk was nearly gone, though a faint aroma from the striped animal was still present, lingering unperceived for several minutes only to torment those nearby by coming forth unexpectedly. Orlena had on a different dress, one more suited to daily life though still far too fine for a ranch.

Seated at the table together for the first time, Norman drew a deep breath, frowned slightly at the smell of skunk and tried to prepare himself for anything. He had never seen his wife and sister together, other than briefly at the station and on the way home. He could tell by a glance at his wife that she wasn't worried, in fact, she looked slightly amused while his sister looked ready to explode.

Hardly waiting until Norman said "Amen," Orlena burst forth, "Norman! You must fire that man!"

Pausing with his glass half way to his lips he asked, "What man?" In the excitement of the skunk he had forgotten about Lloyd's meeting with Orlena.

"Lloyd Something-or-other. He dared to try ordering me about and refused to do as I directed!"

Instead of growing angry or stern as Jenelle had expected, she was amazed to hear his calm reply. "I already did."

Orlena gave a satisfied sigh. She knew Norman would do as she told him to.

"Norman," Jenelle gasped, "you didn't really, did you? He is one of the best hands we have!"

"Oh, I fired him all right," Norman told her. Then, with a grin he added, "But I hired him back not ten seconds later. Of course I wouldn't lose a hand like Hearter."

Before Jenelle could do more than sigh with relief that her husband hadn't dismissed Lloyd, Orlena burst forth in fury.

"You're making fun of me!" she raged, slamming her fork on the table. "You can't keep that impertinent man on this ranch! I won't stand for it. And further more," she stormed, "this place is a disgrace! You have filthy animals, all of whom are ill-tempered, and you don't even care enough about your own sister to order the hired hand," and Orlena spit the words out as though they tasted bad, "to follow my directions! My dress is ruined and you will have to pay for a train ticket for me to go back to the city to have a new one fitted and made and you will pay for the new one too." She sat glaring at her brother as though he was personally responsible for what happened to her dress.

As the angry girl paused for breath, Norman spoke tersely, holding himself sternly in check. "Are you quite through?" he asked. "Because if you are not, perhaps you had better finish all your complaints now before your dinner grows cold."

"Dinner," snorted Orlena. "Grandmother wouldn't have served this to the servants!"

Watching the faces of the angry brother and sister, Jenelle wondered what she could do or say. Should she try to make peace now or would it be better both for Orlena as well as Norman to have it out all at once. Before she could decide, Norman spoke again.

This time his voice was low and stern. "Now it is my turn to talk. In the first place, no one on this ranch is, nor will be, under your orders. At least not until such a time as you can prove yourself worthy of such responsibility. In the second, you will obey any directions given you by anyone working or living here. Third," unintentionally Norman was slowly raising his voice. "Third, the ruined dress was the fault of no one but yourself, and I will not send you nor it to the city. And fourth, if you don't wish to eat your dinner, you may leave and go to your room."

Half a moment of silence followed while the brother and sister locked eyes in a power struggle and the tension in the room mounted higher and higher with each passing second. Then suddenly, Orlena exploded.

"How dare you talk to me like that!" she screamed. "I won't follow anyone's orders like a common slave! And you will pay for a new dress just like that other one!"

"Orlena!"

"And," the spoiled brat pushed back her chair in fury and turned on Jenelle, ignoring her brother, "you are nothing but an ignorant country nobody and you *will* do as I tell you!"

"Orlena!" Norman brought his hand down on the table with a thud, causing the dishes to rattle. "That is enough!" He commanded hotly. "No one speaks to my wife in that manner. Now either apologize this instant or go to your room." His eyes flashed for his temper was roused.

"I won't apologize!" Orlena snapped. "And I—"

Norman interrupted. "Then go to your room. Now!" he thundered, as he saw her open her mouth to speak.

For one brief second, Orlena glared at her brother then turned and ran from the room, up the stairs to her bedroom, the door of which she slammed shut behind her.

In the dining room, Norman gave a sigh that was almost like a groan and leaned back limply in his chair. What had he done? How could he have lost his temper so quickly? Now what should he do?

"It's no use, Jenelle," he frowned. "She can't stay here. I'll have to send her some where else." Leaning his arm on the table and his head in his hand, Norman grew silent.

The ticking of the clock was the only sound to be heard for several minutes. Then in a voice that was soft and gentle, Jenelle spoke, placing a hand on her husband's arm. "Of course you aren't going to send Orlena away, Norman. This is only the first day. She had a trying time with that skunk and isn't used to things around here. I expected an outburst from her of some sort today. She—"

Sitting up, Norman interrupted, "It isn't just Orlena I was thinking of. You saw how it was, I can't keep my temper when she starts talking to you in that manner."

With a little laugh, Jenelle squeezed his arm. "Darling, don't get upset for me, it isn't worth it. Her words aren't going to hurt me."

"Still," Norman put in, "I won't have her speaking to you in that tone of voice or in that manner!"

Seeing that Norman was growing excited again, Jenelle wisely refrained from saying anything further on the subject but started eating as though nothing had happened. She knew her husband well enough to know when he needed time to think.

Slowly, after sitting in silence for some time, Norman too began to eat. There was no light talk at the table that meal, as the Mavrich house was accustomed to, for both were busy with their own thoughts.

It wasn't until the meal was concluded and Jenelle had cleared away the dishes that Norman, following her into the kitchen, spoke.

"You are right. We can't send her away, Sweet. Though she shouldn't speak to you in that manner."

"Of course she shouldn't," Jenelle agreed, looking up into her husband's face. "The problem is, she doesn't know better, so we will have to teach her."

Norman made a rueful face. "I'm not much help, I'm afraid, when I lose my temper. I shouldn't, I know, but when she starts going on like she did . . ."

"You can leave the room if you have to," Jenelle suggested softly.

"And leave you to put up with her? Hardly!"

Jenelle smiled. "Only until you have time to cool off. I don't think it would hurt any of us."

Norman sighed and then spoke, his voice subdued. "I'll have to try it, Sweetheart. But now," he gave another sigh, "I must go talk to Orlena. I have to apologize for losing my temper, but she has to understand she is not in charge of anything here! I won't let her terrorize the entire place as she did at Grandmother's."

"I'll be praying for you," Jenelle whispered softly with a kiss.

Up in her room, Orlena fumed and fussed, muttering to herself and pacing the floor. Why did she have to live here? Norman didn't care for her at all. If he did he would sell this stupid ranch and move to the city! And that sister-in-law was even worse. She didn't even pay any attention to her directions. "She thinks she is better than me. I'll soon put her in her place. And that hired hand," Orlena scowled darkly. "He'll wish he'd never crossed me!"

And so this spoiled, pampered child who had been given every desire and had every wish granted, who had never been made to do what she disliked unless it was her lessons, and had been issuing orders to servants since before she could talk plainly, sulked in her room and vowed to make things go her own way. She was interrupted by a knock on her door.

"Yes," the word was spoken coldly and she wondered if it would be her brother or sister-in-law.

Quietly Norman opened the door and stepped in. His sister gave him no greeting but sat eyeing him with an expression of extreme distaste. This did not make things easier, but with a silent prayer for help, he began to speak.

"How did it go?" Jenelle looked up as Norman entered the kitchen a quarter of an hour later.

Sitting down heavily in a chair, the owner and master of Triple Creek sighed and shook his head. "I don't know. I apologized for losing my temper, but Orlena seemed to think that meant I was giving in to her demands of getting rid of Lloyd and buying her a new absurd dress."

Jenelle finished wringing out her dishcloth and hung it up to dry. Untying her apron, she placed it on the hook behind the door before going over to sit next to her husband. "Did you get her to understand that neither of those things was going to happen?"

"I don't know. She listened, but I don't think she really believed me."

Sympathetically, Jenelle leaned her head on his shoulder and squeezed his hand.

"I don't know what we are going to do about her, Darling, I really don't."

"We can pray for her and love her," Jenelle answered softly.

"Pray, yes. Love her? I hate to admit it, but right now, I

don't know if I do."

"You do," assured his wife positively. "If you didn't, you never would be trying to help her but would send her off tomorrow to some place else."

Giving a shamefaced smile, Norman replied, "You're right. But it's going to be a lot of work."

CHAPTER 7

NOTHING TO WEAR

"Jenelle," Norman paused as he was about to rise from the breakfast table the following morning, "I feel like a shirker leaving you here alone with my sister again. If I didn't have so much to do . . ."

Mrs. Mavrich smiled up at her husband's troubled face. "You are not shirking, Dear," she told him. "You have work that must be done and perhaps Orlena and I can get better acquainted." She almost added, "If you are not here," but said instead, "Her trunk still needs to be unpacked. Do you suppose she has anything to wear that is at all suitable for life here?"

Raising his eyebrows Norman shrugged. "You're asking me? I have no idea what she has except that awful black thing she had on yesterday. What did she wear after her encounter with the skunk?"

At that Jenelle burst into a merry laugh. "Oh, go along with you to the fields. You're about as much help as a cow," and she laughed some more, though her face grew sober as the door shut behind Norman. Did Orlena have anything suitable to wear?

All the time she was clearing away the dishes and doing her morning chores, Jenelle puzzled and pondered over the problem of Orlena's wardrobe. "I really don't think she has anything," she murmured. "I'll have to get to work. I wonder

49

if she would like to go into town with me tomorrow and pick out some material?"

Footsteps were heard and Jenelle turned brightly with a cheery greeting for her young sister. Orlena barely acknowledged it with a slight inclination of the head and remained silent.

Ignoring the silence, Jenelle spoke cordially, completely leaving the previous evening in the past. "You must be hungry," she began. "I've already finished my chores so I'll join you at the table." She carried in Orlena's breakfast and set it before her. "I thought today would be a good day to unpack your trunk. That way Norman can carry it to the attic this evening and you will be all settled in. Perhaps tomorrow you would like to go into town with me to do some shopping. You know," she went on, seemingly oblivious to the silence of the girl across from her, "I think I'll enjoy having another woman about the house. Sometimes I get rather lonesome. Do you enjoy sewing?"

"What kind of sewing?" Orlena asked warily.

"Making clothes and mending."

Orlena looked disgusted. "That is what you pay seamstresses for, or didn't you know that?"

"Yes," Jenelle conceded, ignoring the tone of the girl opposite her, "but I would hope they loved their work, wouldn't you? It always makes it much more enjoyable."

"I embroider," Orlena said suddenly.

Jenelle looked interested at once. "That must be delightful work. I tried it once, but I snarled it up so badly that I couldn't fix it. Since then I've stuck with plain sewing."

Orlena didn't volunteer the fact that her only attempt to embroider anything was a handkerchief on which the red and yellow flowers ended up looking like the flames of a fire more than anything else.

"Now," Jenelle began briskly as Orlena finished her last bite. "Would you rather wipe off the table and sweep the floor or wash up these few dishes?" The question was asked so matter-of-factly, as though Jenelle asked that sort of question everyday and had no thought of either option being a chore, that no one would have guessed just how quickly her heart was beating nor that she braced herself for an explosion.

For a moment Orlena stared at her and then, in a haughty voice replied, "That is work for the servants."

"I don't have any servants. This is such a small house and there really isn't much to do; if I had a servant, she would run out of things to do long before the day was done. And what about me?" here she paused to laugh. "Why, I'd have nothing to do."

For answer, Orlena gave a sniff and rose from the table.

"Orlena," Jenelle's soft voice halted her young sister. "Would you like help unpacking your trunk?"

"Well, I'm certainly not doing it," was the curt reply before Orlena swept out of the room and up the stairs.

"Well!" Jenelle blinked. "That's that. I mustn't push her too much yet. I'll let her grow more used to things around here. Poor child!" She had been busy as she talked to herself, brushing the few crumbs off the table and washing the plate, cup and utensils. After a quick glance at the floor, Jenelle decided it really didn't need to be swept.

Up in her room, Orlena waited for Jenelle's coming. Her feelings were mixed. The unpacking of her trunk meant that she would be staying at the ranch at least until school started, while if it remained unpacked, there was always the possibility of Norman sending her back to the city. Seating herself in the chair, Orlena tapped her foot. One thing was certain, *she* would not unpack a thing. Perhaps the sight of all her fine dresses would impress her brother's country wife.

The kitchen was hot, and Jenelle pushed back her damp hair from her face. She was tired. Supper would be ready soon, Norman was expected any minute and the table wasn't yet set. "I wish I could ask Orlena to set it for me," she sighed reaching into the cupboard for the plates.

"What was that you were muttering about?" a voice

asked behind her as a strong arm turned her around.

"Oh, Norman," Jenelle gave a start and almost dropped a plate. "I didn't hear you come in."

Quickly catching the plate and setting it on the counter, Norman smiled. "So I noticed." And bending his head he kissed the ruby lips before him. "You were talking to yourself again."

"I do that quite often," she retorted, laughing a little and turning to get the other plates and to hide her hot face. "I was just wishing the table would sort of set itself tonight," she confessed. "Because I haven't had time to do it yet."

"Where's Orlena?" Norman stepped over to the door and opening it, glanced through into the empty dining room but saw no sign of his sister.

"Probably getting ready to eat . . ."

"I don't like you working alone in this hot kitchen," he frowned as he saw his wife's flushed cheeks and noticed the dots of perspiration on her temples.

"I've been doing it most of my life," she reminded him quietly.

"But you had your mother to help you," he protested.

Jenelle smiled indulgently. "Not since I married you," she told him, adding, "Don't you think you should be following your sister's example and washing up?"

"All right," he grinned. "I can take a hint. But," he paused in the doorway as another frown crossed his face, "I still don't like it."

Jenelle quickly set three places, and by the time she had the food on the table, Norman and Orlena were waiting. It was a relief to Jenelle to discover that the dining room was cooler than the kitchen had been. She didn't want to admit it even to herself, but she was feeling more tired than she had been for a long time.

Grace was said and the meal began. It was a quiet one. No one seemed inclined to talk much. Perhaps the heat had something to do with it or perhaps everyone felt too tired to spend their energy talking. In either case, the meal was half over before Norman, after several glances at his strangely quiet sister and his tired looking wife, questioned, "Did you two have a busy day?"

Jenelle nodded. "It takes a while to unpack a trunk and get everything set to rights." She didn't add that it took longer doing it alone with an exacting mistress to please. "And that reminds me, Norman, Orlena's trunk is ready to be taken to the attic."

"I can do that after supper," Norman agreed.

Silence again descended until the steady, sure hand of the clock had ticked away three minutes. Then Jenelle spoke. "How was your day, Dear?"

"We're ready to move the cattle from the west creek pasture to the south creek. We'll do that tomorrow."

"Speaking of tomorrow," Jenelle set her glass of water down and pushed her empty plate slightly away. "Orlena and I were thinking of going into town for a few things tomorrow."

"No." Norman spoke quickly, but with quiet decision and Jenelle looked somewhat surprised. "I don't want you, either of you," he added, looking first at his wife and then at his sister, "driving all the way to town in this heat. There won't even be a cloud cover tomorrow. Wait until it cools off somewhat."

Orlena hadn't really wanted to go to town with her sister-in-law, but when Norman had so quickly and adamantly said they couldn't go, she immediately felt contrary. She looked at Jenelle, wondering if she would pout or plead, but was surprised to discover she did neither. There was no sign of even disappointment on Jenelle's still slightly flushed face. And no words of protest came from her mouth. Orlena opened her mouth to put in her own protest, but she had no chance to say anything.

"Oh, Norman, do be careful tomorrow if it is going to be that hot." Jenelle looked concerned.

"We will, Sweet. That is why it will probably take us all day. We'll be moving them slowly."

With a sigh, Jenelle pushed back her chair, signaling that supper was over. There were still the dishes to wash and she dreaded the heat of the kitchen.

Feeling uncertain about the outcome, yet determined not to let his wife work in the hot kitchen alone, Norman spoke quickly. "We'll all help with the dishes tonight. That way they will be done all the sooner."

A grateful look swept over Jenelle's face and she smiled at her husband. Yet, she wondered, will Orlena have anything to say about the arrangement? She didn't have long to wait.

For a full half a minute Orlena was speechless. Had her brother told her they would all be moving out and living with Indians, she couldn't have been more astonished. She help wash dishes? She, Orlena Mavrich, who had had servants all her life, or at least as much of it as she could remember, expected to help in the kitchen like a common maid!

Norman's voice, quick and genial, interrupted her thoughts. "Here Sis, we'll stack the plates and you can carry them out to the kitchen while I grab these serving dishes."

"I will not!" Orlena had found her voice. "I am not your servant!" Her grey eyes flashed.

Norman's voice was even as he replied, "No, you are not. You are a member now of Triple Creek Ranch and each member is expected to carry their share of the load around here."

"I am not a member, I am a guest, and I'll have you remember that!"

Jenelle gave Norman no chance to reply, for she saw that his temper was rapidly rising. "Dear," and she placed a hand on his arm, "just carry those out and put them on the counter for me, won't you?"

And Norman, biting back his sharp words, turned from his sister to the kitchen. After setting the dishes carefully down, he braced his hands on the counter top and stared down at the floor, his heart crying for help. "Oh, God, what do I do?" he pleaded silently. "I can't let Orlena be another burden on Jenelle, but how do I make her help? And most of all, how can I keep my temper with her when she talks like that?" He pushed away from the counter and strode over to stand in the open doorway and stare into the cloudless evening sky with troubled eyes.

Back in the dining room, Orlena still stood with an expression of mingled feelings; anger, pride, annoyance and surprise all mingled together.

Jenelle too had remained in the room after Norman's departure. Her voice was low but steady as she remarked, "No truly polite guest would refuse to assist her hostess in any small way possible." She paused a moment, wondering if her words had even reached the ears of the young, thoroughly spoiled girl before her. Seconds ticked by and then she spoke again, this time in her normal, pleasant voice. "Orlena, would you please carry those plates out to the kitchen for me?" And without waiting to hear or see what Orlena's response would be, Jenelle, having gathered up the remaining dishes, turned and bore them to the kitchen.

Much to her own astonishment, Orlena reached for the plates and followed her sister to the kitchen where she received a gracious thanks.

At the sound of his wife's voice, Norman turned in the doorway and could hardly contain his start of surprise at the sight of his sister holding three dirty dishes.

Feeling that she had pushed things as far as she dared for one night, Jenelle didn't offer an apron to Orlena after she had taken the plates from her.

"Will you excuse me now?" Orlena asked in lofty tones, "I am feeling quite worn out with the exertions of the day and wish to retire."

"Of course," Jenelle smiled. "Thank you, Dear, for your help; it saved me another trip out to the dining room. Good-night."

"Good-night," came the stiff reply and the door to the dining room was shut behind the retreating child.

"Well!" Norman exclaimed, "How did you ever—? But

she should stay and help—"

Here he was interrupted. "Don't push things, Norman," Jenelle advised. "It was a start. We can't expect too much from her all at once."

Picking up a towel, Norman prepared to wipe the dishes as Jenelle washed and rinsed them. Neither one spoke again until the kitchen was clean. Then Norman, taking his wife's arm, gently led her into the front room, which was much cooler than the hot kitchen, and placed her in a chair.

Giving a weary sigh, Jenelle leaned her head back against the cushions. "I don't think I'll want to move again until morning," she murmured.

"Perhaps I should have taken you to bed then," Norman smiled a bit anxiously as he pulled up a chair beside his wife once he had placed a foot stool for her feet.

"I'll be all right once I've rested a bit."

Norman shook his head. "What have you done today," he questioned, "that has made you so tired? Was it my sister?"

Quickly Jenelle shook her head. "She didn't do anything but sit and talk. And, Darling, you were right."

"About what?"

"Orlena talking. The entire time I was unpacking her trunk, she talked about the fabric, the lace, where she first wore the dress and who was at the party she wore the dress to."

"*You* unpacked her trunk?" He knitted his eyebrows together and his face grew stern.

Jenelle bit her lip. She hadn't meant to mention that part. It was too late now. All she could do was to try to smooth things over. "It wasn't strenuous, Norman, and I'm sure Orlena never unpacked a trunk before. Would you hand me my mending?" she asked, trying to change the subject.

"No," he shook his head. "You're not mending tonight and you're not knitting either," he added as she glanced around and moved as though to rise. "You are going to sit in that chair and do nothing more wearing than talking."

Folding her hands, Jenelle addressed the light, "I suppose Mr. Mavrich doesn't care if he has buttons on his shirts or not, and as for that new pair of socks I was knitting him, perhaps I should make them for one of the hands. Lloyd might like them."

A chuckle came from Norman. "That's still not going to get you either basket," he told her. "You've already worked too hard." Then his voice changed. "Did Orlena do anything except talk of clothes while you were doing her work?"

"She directed me about some things," Jenelle replied quietly, wishing Orlena had done something, anything to help unpack that trunk.

"What did you do after the trunk was unpacked?"

"We looked at her black dress which I had rinsed out this morning."

"And?" Norman pressed, frowning at the thought that here was another thing Jenelle had done for Orlena.

"It doesn't look very well. The lace is in tatters most places and as for the train, it might as well be used for a rag. I can take the dress apart and make another not so fancy, though it will still be out of place for this ranch."

"Did my sister have anything to say about the state her dress was in?"

"Plenty," was the somewhat reluctant reply. "But," she added quickly as Norman was about to speak, "let's not talk about that. The dress can't be worn as it is and Orlena knows it."

"Then tell me what you did after the dress had been examined and its past glories made much of and its destruction blamed on those who had nothing to do with it."

A smile flickered across Jenelle's face at Norman's perception. How well her husband knew his sister, even if he hadn't seen much of her for the past eight years. "Then I went to begin supper and Orlena went her own way. But, Darling," her voice sparkled as she looked across to her husband, "did you know that Mrs. Stolburg has a dress made out of the very same material as one which hangs this very minute in Orlena's closet?"

Norman's face wore a blank expression. "Huh?"

Bursting into rippling laughter, Jenelle didn't reply right away. "It's true, Dear," she assured him at last, "Orlena informed me of that fact this morning."

Norman wasn't impressed. "Humph. The question is, does she have anything that will work on this ranch?"

"No, not a thing."

Drumming his fingers on the arm of his chair, Norman fell silent. His eyes held a far away look in them and his wife waited. "Perhaps," he at last began slowly, when Jenelle was about to suggest they retire for the night, "it will be cooler on Monday and we can go into town then. I suppose we can't ask her to do much with the costumes she has now, can we?"

Jenelle shook her head, feeling pity around her heart for her husband, for his shoulders drooped and he looked so bewildered about the whole situation. "Darling," she leaned forward letting her hand rest lightly on his arm, "can we not spend some time right now praying for Orlena and asking our Heavenly Father for wisdom in dealing with her?"

Kneeling side by side, Mr. and Mrs. Mavrich brought all their worries and cares for their sister to Him who cares for each one, asking for wisdom of whom it was said, "if any man lacks wisdom let him ask of God who giveth to all," and pleading for true love from the One who is Love. When they at last rose, Norman held his wife close in his arms and murmured with his cheek pressed against her light hair, "I thank God for giving me the most wonderful wife in the world."

T

CHAPTER 8

POOR ORLENA

Saturday passed quietly enough. Jenelle, busy with her usual household duties, refrained from asking her young sister to assist her. Not that she wouldn't have welcomed help, but she was too busy to deal with the storm which would have surely come had she asked. Besides, she didn't feel as though the time of confrontation had arrived. "I'll wait until we get new material." She spoke softly as she moved about upstairs getting the rooms to right. "She can help sew her dresses."

Orlena, having no desire to venture forth in the great outdoors after her last experience, wandered about the house until, discovering a bookshelf, she established herself in a chair and began to read. True, none of the books were quite to her liking, but there were enough of them to keep her occupied most of the day.

The evening meal passed by quietly enough. Norman told about moving the cattle and Jenelle refrained from mentioning anything too specific about her day with Orlena. Orlena got out of carrying any dishes to the kitchen on plea of a headache.

The sun was barely up the next morning when Orlena was roused by someone shaking her shoulder gently and a voice calling her name.

"What do you want?" she asked rather startled, for

Jenelle was standing beside the bed.

"This is Sunday morning, Orlena, and since we have to leave for church in a little over an hour, breakfast will be on the table in five minutes."

Yawning, Orlena sat up. It took her a few minutes to really wake up enough to let Jenelle's words register in her brain. When they finally did, her sister-in-law had already slipped away. "Church?" Orlena muttered. "Out here in the middle of nowhere? Who will see us?" To her, church was the place you went to show off your finest clothes, newest hat or latest style of dress. It was also the place to discover the latest fashions and to see if Mrs. DeNae would wear a new hat again.

Standing before her closet, Orlena remembered that her best black dress was ruined. How could she go to church in anything else? She remembered she hadn't gone to church the Sunday after it had been finished. "Now I can't show that horrid Clare Brighten that I loved my grandmother more than she ever loved hers." Her lips pouted as she pulled out another black dress and flung it on the bed. "I'll have to wear black," she thought. "I'm in mourning. But I should have my other one. If Norman hadn't been so unkind about getting my real mourning dress remade, I would be wearing it."

After managing to array herself in the black dress with its many buttons, she brushed her hair, carefully arranging her ringlets in the latest style. This took her much longer with no one to help her and breakfast was half way over before she entered the dining room.

She saw her brother look up at her entrance, exchange a glance with his wife and then return his eyes to his half empty plate as he remarked, "Good Morning, Orlena."

"Morning?" she sniffed, as she settled her flounces in her chair, "It is still practically night."

Norman refrained from answering her and Jenelle remarked about the clouds which had come up over night. The rest of the breakfast was eaten in silence and then Norman departed to hitch up the horses.

The ride to church was an entirely new experience for Miss Orlena. The dust from the horses hooves and the carriage's wheels settled over the fine silk of her black dress turning it nearly grey. The sun was also quite warm for so early in the day, though the clouds did lessen its heat. Long before they reached town Orlena wished she had worn anything but her long sleeve, rather heavy, black dress. Tiny rivers of perspiration trickled down her neck, under her collar and then down her back. Upon arriving at the little country church at last, Orlena gasped. This was nothing at all like she had expected. Where were the stained glass windows? Where was the soft carpet and the cushions in the pews? It was a disgrace. A perfect disgrace. Had Norman been paying the least bit of attention to her at the moment, she would have ordered him to take her to the train station and send her home right away. Fortunately, however, he was speaking with someone and his sister had no choice but to follow Jenelle down the aisle. This she did with her head high and her nose tipped up. She knew she was causing a sensation with her dress and her fine hat, and, if the truth be told, she thoroughly enjoyed it.

Orlena didn't hear a word of the sermon that morning, for her eyes were busy taking in every detail of the small, country church and her mind was calculating just how much the dresses and hats which she could see before her cost and comparing them in her mind to her own wardrobe. Her lip curled slightly at the thought of the difference between them. Orlena had never been taught to think of much else besides herself and money and had never learned the joy of loving Jesus and serving Him; she had never even known of anyone who followed their Savior in their daily life, except Mrs. O'Connor, until her grandmother's death had brought her to Triple Creek Ranch.

Even if Orlena didn't hear the sermon, Norman and Jenelle did, and were helped.

"Thou hast planted my feet on the Rock and established my goings." Mr. Kirby read the text once more.

"If your feet are planted on the Rock of Jesus Christ," he said, "your goings, your ways, yes, and even the trials which seem so hard to bear, have been placed before you by a loving Saviour that your faith might be established more firmly. So, if you feel overwhelmed by life, go to your Rock, that Rock in a weary land which cannot change, go to Him for strength and He will establish you."

T

On Monday, Norman drove his wife and sister into town to do some shopping. He had some things to pick up for the ranch as well. Normally Hardrich or Lloyd or one of the other hands would have made the necessary trip for supplies, but Mr. Mavrich didn't trust his sister's temper, therefore, he went himself.

It was several hours before the trio returned to the ranch, leaving busy tongues to talk in town about Triple Creek's newest member. Orlena had made it very clear that she disapproved of nearly everything she saw. Having discovered that no rich silks or expensive real lace were to be had in the small store, she left everything up to Jenelle, merely sniffing when asked an opinion and remarking that "it might do for a servant or a cook."

Jenelle had been much relieved when Norman had left them to do their own shopping while he did his, for she was afraid some of his sister's remarks would not have settled well with him. It was difficult to deal with Orlena, Jenelle admitted that, but she also realized the wisdom of a quiet answer, or in some cases, no answer at all.

Being too tired to work on new clothes when they returned, Jenelle laid aside the material for another day.

"I wonder if Orlena will enjoy sewing her own clothes?" Mrs. Mavrich mused while she drew the curtains in the front room to shut out the afternoon sun. Then another thought struck her and she paused. How could she have forgotten that today was the day the entire ranch ate together? What would Orlena think of eating with the ranch hands? Should she tell her or wait and let her find out when it was time to eat?

"Perhaps it would be best to wait. At least for the time being." Jenelle sighed and brushed a few stray pieces of hair off her face. Brightening suddenly, she smiled. "I'll have help with the meal tonight at least," she whispered.

She wouldn't have admitted it to anyone, but the fierce heat, as well as the extra work and stress her young sister was causing, had made her more tired than she had been for a while. Tonight would be different for on Monday nights Al St. John, the bunk house cook came to lend a hand. Al also worked with the others, but when it came to cooking, all the hands agreed that no one, with the exception of Mrs. Mavrich, could cook like big St. John.

Out in the fields, Norman turned to his husky field hand and crew chef. "St. John, be sure you don't let my wife do much cooking tonight. She's worn out."

"How am I supposed to do that, Boss, when she's the one in charge?"

There was a general smile among the ranch hands, for it was a well known fact that since Norman Mavrich had brought his wife to the Triple Creek, things about the house had been under the management of Mrs. Mavrich. No one had ever complained, for Jenelle ran the house smoothly and treated the men as friends not just as hired hands.

After thinking a minute, Norman spoke. "I'll send Hearter to help out and you can tell Mrs. Mavrich I said for her to take it easy."

Al St. John nodded and grinned. "I can do that, Boss." Then he turned to his future assistant. "How good are you at scrubbin' taters?" he asked.

"Don't know," Lloyd retorted, pushing back his hat. "Never scrubbed 'em. I just ate 'em, dirt an' all."

A roar of laughter greeted this comeback before the hands returned to their work.

Thus it was that Jenelle, attired in her kitchen apron with her sleeves rolled up, turned around in surprise as not only Al came in, but Lloyd too. St. John delivered Mr. Mavrich's message and Jenelle smiled. She understood and appreciated her husband's kindness in sending extra kitchen help.

"If you both work on the meal," she complained with a laugh, "what will I do?"

The two men looked at each other in confusion. How were they to know what the lady of the house should do?

Smiling at their bewilderment, Jenelle put them at ease by saying, "I'll tell you what, I'll set the table and if you should need anything, you can let me know."

It was while Jenelle was setting the table that Orlena walked in.

"Why are you setting so many places?" Orlena asked. "No one told me there was a party tonight."

Jenelle continued to lay the napkins carefully at each place as she answered, "It is no party, Orlena. Every Monday night everyone on the ranch eats supper together. It is a tradition your grandmother's brother started before Norman came to live with him."

"Humph," Orlena snorted, and then continued almost under her breath, "no wonder he has such ridiculous notions. Consorting with the hired help during meal times! Well," she said aloud, not realizing that her low toned remarks had also reached the ears of her sister, "you needn't set a place for me, for I don't associate socially with hired help." Then she brushed past her sister-in-law and swept to the doorway where she paused and looked back. "Have my supper served to me in my room."

She had nearly reached the top of the stairs when a quiet voice stopped her.

"Orlena."

The girl paused and turned her head, looking down to see Jenelle standing below her at the bottom of the stairs. "Yes?" her voice was haughty and annoyed.

"The choice of eating with the rest of us is up to you; however, the choice of serving meals to you in your room is up to me." Jenelle's voice was calm, even a bit cool as she went on, "And I say that no meals will be served to you in your room tonight. If you wish to eat, you may come to the dining room." Then quietly, with no show of haste or display of temper, Jenelle slipped away.

Orlena watched her go with her mouth partway open to reply, but Jenelle's disappearance gave her no chance to speak. For a moment she remained where she was, then with a "Well! I never!" she continued on to her room where she shoved the door shut with a bang, dropped into her chair with a huff and scowled at the wallpaper as though it were to blame for everything.

To say that Orlena was annoyed at her sister would have been true, she was also annoyed and angry at her brother for letting his wife treat her with such disrespect, seeming to forget the things she had said to Jenelle; she was also confused and astonished. Here she had been at the ranch for six days and never had she heard Jenelle's voice raised nor seen her act upset about a thing. Also, it was puzzling how this same sister-in-law had a way of saying things and then leaving the room before a fitting retort could be made. "She hasn't any courage," Orlena muttered. "If she had she would stay and listen to me." Suddenly she sat up straighter and her eyes glowed. "That is it," she announced triumphantly to her reflection in the mirror, "the next time my brother's wife walks out on me, I will follow her and make her listen to what I have to say! No one in proper society would do what she does. It just goes to show what a selfish, ignorant child she is," and Miss Orlena Mavrich tossed her head, making her curls swing and bounce. "And as for Norman," she snorted her disgust, "he is no gentleman. Expecting me to be happy in the middle of nowhere with no one but a common country housekeeper to talk to! Why Mrs. O'Connor had more manners than Jenelle does!" And so, this poor, spoiled child sat justifying her actions and condemning others until she heard her brother's footsteps on the stairs. Yes, she was poor. Not poor in the sense that the world counts, for she had money enough waiting for her to come of age, but she was poor because she knew not the love that comes truly from the heart, poor because real happiness had never been known among the riches and splendor of her life, poor, for her friends had only wanted the wealth she lavished among them and the hint of reflected glory she allowed them to bask in, poor for each thought she had was of and about herself. Has anyone known someone who seemed so intent upon themselves that they shut out all real love and happiness to hold onto the one thing they cherish most, their pride? Orlena's pride was her most prized possession and thus the enemy of souls used it to rule her life and gave her no peace.

Flinging open her door, she was about to call to her brother and inform him of the impertinence of his wife, but to her utter disgust, Jenelle's gay laughter sounded in her ears. Silently she pulled the door shut, moved to the window and stood looking out.

When Norman's voice called to her some fifteen minutes later to ask if she were going down, she replied shortly, "No," and then added in lower tones, "I won't eat with hired help like common country people."

Scowling, Orlena watched the men striding from the bunk house laughing and talking in the greatest of good humor. "Ignorant nobodies," she muttered. "This place is worse than the slums of the city and I won't stay here much longer." The only things that kept her from packing and walking away right then was her trunk in the attic and the fact that she didn't know where she would go since school didn't start for another few months. The only things? There was something else keeping her at Triple Creek Ranch though Orlena Mavrich didn't know it. Every day earnest prayers had been made for her from nearly every member of the busy ranch. Norman and Jenelle never went to bed without spending time on their knees pleading for this younger sister to find the only Fountain of lasting Joy and the One who is Love. Those prayers, and a Father's tender plan, kept Orlena at Triple Creek Ranch.

T

CHAPTER 9

WHAT CAN SHE DO?

No one at the supper table that night mentioned the fact or even seemed to notice that a member of the ranch wasn't eating with them. Jenelle had simply told Norman in their room that Orlena had declined to eat supper that night and he wisely asked no questions. The meal was delightful as it always was and the talk merry and light. Many a time hearty laughter rang out and floated up to the still pouting Orlena, who in her wounded pride thought they must be laughing about her and fumed at the idea.

At last, as the sun prepared to drop out of sight behind the hills, Orlena, watching from the window, saw the hired hands leaving in small groups heading for the bunkhouse, and gradually all grew quiet. Still she remained at the open window, a warm, evening breeze blowing gently against her flushed cheeks; the stars came out one by one and twinkled down at her while the gentle sounds of the horses in the corrals, the leaves softly whispering, the evening chirps of the birds all contrived together to soothe the ruffled spirits of the child. The sights and sounds of the peaceful night brought calm to Orlena at last, causing her anger to die down. Slowly she began to get ready for bed, lighting no lamp and giving no response to Jenelle's quiet tap on the door. She was tired and worn out. She felt as though her whole world had turned up-side-down and she was somehow trapped beneath it.

When Orlena came down to her late breakfast in the morning, she spoke not a word but ate in silence and then sat staring into space. Jenelle was puzzled. What had come over her sister? Was she only tired from the shopping of yesterday? Was she not feeling well? Whatever the cause, Jenelle enjoyed the quiet.

It wasn't until later in the morning that Jenelle, with many inward misgivings but with outward calmness and a matter of fact tone, came to her young sister's room and said, "Orlena, let's go start work on one of your new dresses. I'm sure the pattern will fit you but I would like to try it before we cut it out. We will go to the parlor as it is cooler down there."

Orlena followed without a word and stood still while Jenelle measured her, but, when Jenelle had cut out the bodice and had directed Orlena to baste it together, she found her tongue.

"I will not," she declared haughtily. "I am not a sewing girl."

Jenelle was quite calm, even a trifle amused when she replied, "Of course you are not. No one would think of such a thing. Around here everyone does their own sewing except the menfolk," and here Jenelle paused to laugh at the idea. "But since you will be the one wearing the dress, you can help sew it."

"I didn't say I needed a new dress."

"No, you didn't." It was mildly put. "But as nothing you have now is quite suited for ranch life, I took it for granted that a new dress or two would be of use."

Orlena snorted. "Well, if you are anxious to make these dresses," she gave the material a look of scorn, "you can sew them yourself." With that she turned to leave the room but her sister-in-law's voice stopped her.

"Orlena, these dresses will be made, and you will help sew them."

"I'd like to see you try and make me!" Orlena snapped.

"You will start on the bodice." Had Jenelle sounded the

least bit angry she would have flown into a passion and continued out of the room, but the quiet and positive words "you will" left Orlena rather bewildered and astonished. Could Jenelle really make her sew? She turned and stared at her sister. There was no sign of anger in her face, but there was a look of something else, something strong and determined, forceful even, though Orlena couldn't think of the small Mrs. Mavrich as forceful. Hesitantly, she waited.

Jenelle wasted no time. Handing Orlena the bodice and a needle and thread, she nodded towards the sofa by the open window. "Over there I'm sure would be a pleasant place to sew. There is enough light but the hot sun won't be directly on you." Her voice was quiet even friendly and much to her own astonishment, Orlena found herself moving over and sitting down on the sofa. She was actually going to sew!

The morning was rather trying to both sisters, for Orlena really didn't know how to sew and Jenelle was forced to try to teach her, along with working on her own sewing. After two hours of work, Jenelle thanked Orlena for her help and folded up the sewing. She had had enough for one morning.

That evening as Jenelle brushed her long, light hair, she told her husband about the day, mentioning that she and Orlena had spent some time that morning sewing.

Norman looked up, pausing in the midst of pulling off a boot. "Orlena sewed?" He questioned in astonishment. "How did you get her to do it?"

Jenelle kept her face turned away as she replied lightly, "Oh, I didn't force her to. But Norman, she really doesn't know how to sew."

Putting his boot down beside its mate, Mr. Mavrich stood up and, moving over beside his wife, turned her around so he could look into her face. "How did you get my sister to sew?" he repeated.

"I simply told her she had to sew, and she did it."

"Uh huh, that's all." Norman raised his eyebrows in skepticism. "You didn't threaten her?"

"Norman!" Jenelle exclaimed indignantly. "Of course I didn't. I simply told her she would help sew the dresses, and I think she did just because she was too astonished to know what else to do."

He shook his head. "I don't see how you do it, Darling. If I tell her to do something she loses her temper and won't do it. But you tell her to do something and she does it." He kissed her gently. "You certainly are a wonder."

Jenelle laughed softly. "I didn't do anything special," she protested. "Norman." She looked up into his face, a worried expression in her eyes. "Did you notice Orlena was extra quiet tonight?"

His arms slid around her and she was pulled close to him. "No, I can't say that I did. Why?"

Fiddling with the buttons on his shirt, Jenelle spoke slowly, not quite sure how to say what was bothering her. "Orlena hardly said one word all morning," she began, "until I told her she had to help sew, and then after she had started she scarcely spoke. She didn't talk at all while we ate tonight. Norman," she raised her eyes to meet his, "do you think she's feeling all right?"

"Most likely," he replied easily. "I don't think she would hesitate to make it known if she wasn't. Perhaps she just ran out of things to complain about." He bent and kissed her. "Don't worry about her, Sweet. Tomorrow you'll probably be wishing she would stop talking again."

Norman was right, for the following morning Orlena again found reason for complaint and when Jenelle brought up the sewing, Orlena tossed her head. "I've decided," she remarked airily, "that I was not brought up to be a sewing girl."

Jenelle looked at her with interest. "Were you brought up to cook? Or would you rather gather the eggs and feed the chickens?"

"I was brought up to be a lady, not a farm drudge."

"Suppose we discuss this as we sew," Mrs. Mavrich wisely suggested, and so, Orlena found herself sewing once more. This time her tongue was not silent, and Jenelle was thankful her husband wasn't there to listen.

It was a tiring morning to Jenelle, and after dinner she retired to her room with a headache, leaving Orlena to her own devices. She didn't mean to sleep, only to rest a little while before starting supper, but the next thing she knew, someone was calling her name in low tones.

Upon opening her eyes she saw Norman's anxious face gazing down into hers. "What time is it?" she yawned.

"A little after five."

"Oh!" Jenelle exclaimed, starting up and then putting a hand to her throbbing head. "I haven't even started supper yet. What are you doing here?"

Gently Norman pushed his wife back onto the pillows and sat down beside her. "We were all coming back and I couldn't find you downstairs. Orlena was reading and said you had gone to your room after dinner. Are you all right? You look pale."

"I'll be all right. It's just a headache, but I must get up and start supper." However, when she tried to sit up, the pain in her head made her dizzy and she dropped back.

"Darling! What is it?" Norman was alarmed. He had never seen Jenelle quite like this before. "I'll have someone ride for Dr. French."

Jenelle put up a hand and caught his sleeve. "No, Norman. I think it was the heat, and I've been a little extra tired these last few days. Don't fret about me." She smiled faintly into his worried eyes. "But what will we do about your supper?"

"St. John always makes more than enough over at the bunk house. Orlena and I can eat there. But what about you?"

"Just some tea and toast is all I want."

Norman bent over and dropped a kiss on her forehead.

"I'll have Orlena make some for you and bring it up."

"Norman," Jenelle smiled faintly, "I'm sure Orlena hasn't the least idea how to make either one. Remember she was brought up in the city."

At this Norman sighed and, stepping over to the window, drummed his fingers lightly on the sill. "Well," he said at last, "I'd make your tea and toast for you, but I'm afraid it wouldn't be eatable. Cooking just isn't in my line. But, I'll find someone." Turning back to the bed he left another kiss and spoke softly, "Now get some more rest. I think I need to have a talk with my sister." He muttered the last half to himself, but Jenelle heard him.

"Be patient, Dear," Jenelle pleaded. "Remember, she has only been here a week."

"I will, Sweet." And Norman slipped from the room.

As he started down the hall, he thought, "Orlena has got to start doing something towards pulling her own weight. I won't have my wife exhausted because of the extra work Orlena makes." He felt his temper rise and he paused. "This won't work. I can't go talk with her if I'm already worked up. It'd be best to talk to St. John first."

The big, Triple Creek Ranch cook was more than happy to provide his boss and Orlena with their supper. His concern for Mrs. Mavrich was only equaled by the concern of the rest of the hands, for Mrs. Mavrich was a friend to them all.

Pausing in his return to the house, Norman changed directions and headed instead to the barn. There in the shadow of a secluded corner, he knelt and prayed for wisdom and patience in dealing with his sister. The task before him was not one to his liking, but he knew it must be done sooner or later. At last he rose and walked purposefully towards the house. Halting at the door, he drew in a deep breath, squared his shoulders and stepped in.

"Well, there he goes," Hearter remarked, standing

before a window in the bunk house.

"Who?" Hardrich queried.

"Mr. Mavrich. I don't envy him!" And Lloyd shook his head, turning away.

"I don't think anyone does, but," and the ranch foreman looked about the room, "I think he could use some prayer right now. He looked worn out."

T

CHAPTER 10

SETTING THINGS STRAIGHT

Norman felt tired as he thought of talking to his sister, but having once made up his mind to do something that needed to be done, he wasn't the sort of man to back out of it no matter how difficult it was.

Finding Orlena in the cool parlor curled up on a chair with a book as he had left her, Norman drew a deep breath, dropped into a nearby chair and began.

"Orlena, we need to talk about some things."

Curiously, Orlena looked up from her book. Norman wanted to talk? She wondered what it was about. Aloud she said, "I hope it is about my future for there is only so much a person of good breeding can stand."

"It is about your future," he agreed, unsure quite how to go about it, for he didn't want another explosion to occur as it had in the city. "You have now been at the Triple Creek Ranch for a week. Jenelle and I have tried to make things easy so you could have a chance to adjust yourself, but now you will have to start pulling your own weight. To begin with," he went on quickly for he saw that his sister seemed about to speak. "To begin with, you will eat breakfast with us each morning. Jenelle doesn't have the time to prepare breakfast for you at all hours of the morning. She has enough to do without that. Second, you will be expected to do a few chores about the place, either in the house or outside. Which chores they will be I will leave up to you and Jenelle."

Norman paused, collecting his thoughts, and before he could speak again, Orlena broke the silence.

"That is what you think," she flashed, shutting her book with a thud. "Well, I will have you know a few things, Norman Mavrich, which you seem to have forgotten. In the first place, I am not your servant nor a hired hand! I am a guest, granddaughter and sole heir of the late Mrs. Marshall Mavrich, and I was not bred to be a ranch drudge. Secondly, I will not be staying here long enough to be bothered by chores. As soon as the new term opens at Madam Viscount's Seminary I will be leaving here and will hereafter spend my vacations with my friends unless you decide to leave this place and live in the city like you should. Have I made myself clear?" Nothing could have been more haughty than Miss Orlena Mavrich's voice, nor more regal than the toss of her brown ringlets as she looked at her brother with raised eyebrows.

"Perfectly."

"Then there is nothing more to be said, is there?" and Orlena opened her book once more.

"Actually there is more to be said." Norman's jaw squared and his shoulders straightened. It appeared to be another battle of wills and Norman was determined not to lose it. "You are right when you say you are the granddaughter of Mrs. Marshall Mavrich; however, you are not her sole heir, and until you reach the age of twenty-one, which is not for another nine years, I am your legal guardian and will decide where you will live, where you will attend school and what you are to do. And you may as well know now that you will not be going back to that seminary this school term nor any other term. No," he held up his hand as his sister again opened her mouth. "Let me finish. When you say you are not a servant nor a hired hand, you are right. You are a member of the Triple Creek Ranch and as a member you have certain responsibilities. You have claimed that you were not bred to be a ranch drudge. Neither was I. Don't forget Orlena that I am your brother and the only son and heir of Marshall Norman Mavrich and spent the first twelve years of my life attending the finest schools back east before we moved to Blank City. When Mother and Father had to go abroad on business, I spent a year out here on Triple Creek with Uncle Hiram. I returned to the city once our parents returned and there I was tutored for two years. After our parents' death I was sent to live out here with Uncle Hiram where I worked and learned until I was able to send myself to college where I graduated second in my class." Norman was not one who boasted about his accomplishments, and few references did he ever make of his childhood, but now it was different. If Orlena thought living on a ranch meant one was an ignorant person, he would be happy to enlighten her.

For a moment after he stopped talking, Orlena simply stared at him. She had never known her brother was a college graduate. True she had never inquired into it. But if Norman was so well educated, why had he married Jenelle and why on earth had he stayed on this stupid ranch? Shutting her book again she pushed her feet off the chair to the floor and faced her brother. "If you have so much knowledge," she snorted, "why did you ruin the honored family name by marrying an ignorant country nobody and continuing to live out in the middle of nowhere?"

The mention of Jenelle in those belittling tones brought a flash to Norman's eyes and a set to his jaw that the few troublemakers in town knew too well. He swallowed hard and struggled to keep his voice low and steady. "If you think that Jenelle is an ignorant country nobody, you had better think again. She attended Sheldon's Academy for young ladies, speaks three foreign languages fluently, and is a descendent of a French nobleman. As for living out here, it is because I happen to greatly enjoy the freedom of the great outdoors, and working on a ranch is something I enjoy. Now is there anything else you wish me to explain to you?

"If there is nothing else, perhaps we should prepare for our dinner. We will be eating in the bunkhouse with the men tonight since Jenelle is not feeling well."

Then Orlena's indignation come forth in a burst. Her book fell to the floor with a thud as she sprang to her feet and placed her hands on her hips. "I will tell you what I told your wife. I do not associate socially with hired help!"

Norman had risen also and now stood facing his angry sister. "Would you rather not eat?" he questioned quietly.

"I would rather starve than eat with the help!" she snapped.

"So be it then," and Norman turned to go.

"Norman Mavrich, don't you dare leave until I'm through talking!" Orlena stamped her foot.

Turning, Norman regarded her with a feeling of irritation and anger struggling for mastery. "I wasn't aware that you had anything left to say." His voice was low and he could feel his temper slowly rising. He sent up a swift though silent prayer for help and waited.

Orlena was furious. All the emotions which had been stewing inside her for several days had risen, and seeing her brother's outwardly calm face only added to her wrath. He didn't care a thing about her or he would never calmly tell her she could starve! All he cared about was himself, his darling wife and his precious ranch. Well, she would set him straight!

"What more do you want to say, Orlena?" Norman broke into her thoughts. "Please say them quickly for even if you don't wish to eat, I am quite hungry."

"Of course that is all you care about. All that matters to you is that you have everything your own way. You don't even make your hired help treat your own sister with respect and let your wife speak rudely to me when I have done nothing."

Norman's eyebrows shot up, "Jenelle, speak rudely?"

"Yes, Jenelle, your precious wife, who it appears, in your eyes, can do no wrong has rudely spoken to me and forced me to do things which are disagreeable because she won't spend the money to hire someone else to do them. She seems to think that I've come to be her personal slave and I tell you I won't stand for it any longer!" Again she stamped her foot.

"What things did my wife make you do, Orlena?" Norman's eyes flashed but he managed to keep his voice quiet though his hands clenched and unclenched at his sides.

"Sewing! Now fetch my trunk from the attic; I wish to pack tonight. Then tomorrow you may take me to the train. I'm going to Madam Viscount's and will board there until school starts."

Instead of replying, Norman strode across the room and stared out the window. For several minutes the only sound in the room was the ticking of the small clock on the mantle in the front room. Then the sound of a dinner bell rang through the still room where the brother and sister stood, each waiting a move or word from the other. At last Norman turned. When he spoke, his voice was still low. "We will discuss this after supper. Are you coming to eat?"

For answer Orlena gave a snort and glared at her brother's back when, without another word or look at her, he walked from the room and she heard the kitchen door shut.

Left alone Orlena paced about the room muttering, and then giving way to the hunger and the loneliness which pressed upon her, she burst into tears.

It was with heavy steps and a troubled heart that Norman walked to the bunkhouse. How could he cope with a sister who was as spoiled as Orlena? Would it not be better to send her to some good school? "Pushing your work off onto someone else," his conscience chided. Perhaps he should let her go to Madam Viscount's Seminary this coming term, if she did her share of work now. "Rescue Orlena from herself, I beg you." The words from his grandmother's letter rang through his mind. "No," he muttered, "I will not send my sister to that school! I've seen the 'young ladies' they turn out!"

Someone touched his arm.

He gave a start and looked up quickly. Lloyd was

standing beside him at the door.

"Is Mrs. Mavrich worse, sir? Should I ride for the doc?"

Norman managed a slight smile. "No. Thanks though, Hearter. I was just thinking."

"Must be some heavy thinking the way your shoulders stoop and with that frown on your face," Hardrich said, motioning to an empty chair near him at the long table.

Sitting down in the offered chair, Norman sighed. "You're right. It was pretty heavy."

St. John brought in a plate of food for the ranch boss and joined the others at the table. There was no talking for several minutes as the men ate hungrily. Even Norman forgot his worries momentarily, but they came back in full force with the continued silence.

"Boss?"

Norman turned, "Sorry, St. John, what were you asking?

"Isn't your sister coming?"

"No."

Again silence filled the room except for the sound of knives and forks. Norman didn't notice the glances exchanged between the men around the table but ate without thinking about what he was doing. Had his plate held sawdust and water instead of mashed potatoes and gravy, it is doubtful he would have noticed. Conversations sprang up among the men as the keen edge of hunger was dulled. But Norman, usually one of the men, full of talk and plans, was silent.

"Mr. Mavrich!"

Blinking, Norman looked up. Every eye was fastened on him, some questioningly, others with concern. He smiled wryly. "Sorry, men. That's the third time, isn't it? Was someone talking to me?"

"St. John just asked if you would like more to eat," Hardrich replied. Then he added in a lower tone after Norman had declined seconds, "Is it something you can share, sir?"

Norman hesitated a moment before replying. "Walk with me to the house." Then aloud, "I need to get some tea and toast made for Jenelle, but—" he looked around rather helplessly.

"I'd make her some, but tea just isn't in my line," St. John apologized.

"I'll go make it, sir, if it's all right." Lloyd shoved back his chair and stood up. "My mother always told me I made a good cup of tea."

"I'd be much obliged if you would, Hearter," Norman nodded. "I'll meet you over at the house in a few minutes."

"Mr. Mavrich, sir," Alden said as Norman and Hardrich moved towards the door after the young ranch hand, "Please tell Mrs. Mavrich we're all sorry to hear she's feeling poorly."

An echo seemed to go around the table at Alden's words and Norman smiled a real smile for the first time that evening. "Thanks men. I'll tell her."

Walking slowly towards the ranch house, Norman poured out his trouble into the sympathetic ears of his older foreman. Somehow, just sharing his problem and feeling the pressure of his rough hand on his arm and hearing his quietly spoken words, "I'll be praying for you," lifted Norman's spirit.

"Thanks for listening, Jim. You've been a real friend since my uncle passed away."

Jim Hardrich smiled quietly. "I may not have the answers for you, but you know where to find them. And don't think you're in this alone. We're praying for you and the missus out in the bunk house every night."

There was no time for more words for Lloyd stepped from the kitchen door. "The tray is ready, Mr. Mavrich."

"Thanks, Lloyd. I know Jenelle will be thankful I didn't make it." He held out his hand to each of the men and entered the house with lighter steps. He couldn't ask for a better group of hands to work with.

CHAPTER 11

RESULTS OF TEMPER

Carrying the tray upstairs, he quietly entered the bedroom to find Jenelle awake. "How are you feeling?" he asked softly, setting down the tray.

"A little better. Don't tell me you made the tea," Jenelle half pleaded, half questioned.

"No, Hearter did. Made the toast too. And the men at the bunk house send their regards and hope you're feeling better soon."

Jenelle smiled.

Neither one spoke much as she ate her toast and drank her tea. Jenelle was too tired and Norman's thoughts too occupied.

"Thank you, Norman," Jenelle whispered as she lay back on her pillow after her simple repast was finished. "Now what are you going to do?"

"Do?" Norman bent and kissed his wife, picked up the tea tray and sighed. "Go and finish my talk with Orlena. At least," he added, "if she hasn't gone to bed yet."

"How is it going?"

"I'm not sure, Darling, I'm not sure."

No light had been turned up in the parlor and the light from the setting sun cast a rosy glow on the room. At first glance Norman thought his sister had gone up to her room,

85

but upon a second look he noticed her curled up in the same chair with her face towards the window. He wondered what she was thinking. Could her mood have softened? How should he reopen the conversation?

Clearing his throat softly, Norman entered the room. Orlena didn't move. "I'm sorry if I took a while, Sis," he said gently. "I had to take Jenelle's tea and toast up to her room."

The voice that replied from the depths of the armchair was cool and calm, too calm, Norman thought. "No matter, just fetch my trunk from the attic. And if Jenelle isn't up to packing my trunk tomorrow, you can ride over or send one of your men to fetch the girl who was here when I arrived. She probably doesn't know much about packing, but I will supervise. I suppose you have a train schedule?" Without waiting for a reply nor turning her head from the window, the child continued, "Find out when the next train leaves for Stockton or Blank City. Perhaps it would be better to go to Blank City after all, for then I can get my wardrobe refurnished. I suppose all Grandmother's money is in the bank in my name? I'll have to use some for my clothes."

When she at last paused for breath or perhaps because she had run out of the things she had planned to say, there was a brief moment when the ticking of the clock and the evening twitter of the birds could be heard.

Sighing, Norman leaned wearily back on the sofa. He wished he didn't have to disturb the peace of the evening, but— and here he interrupted his own thoughts. It would be far better to interrupt one evening than to disrupt many days because he put off what needed to be said.

"Orlena, the money Grandmother left you is in a trust fund in my name and you won't have access to it until you are of age. As for train schedules, there is no need of one for no one is going anywhere and I will not bring your trunk down. I told you once, but perhaps you didn't hear me. You will not be going back to Madam Viscount's Seminary, ever." Norman had kept his voice calm but, as he went on, it became more and more firm and that last word had such a definite tone of finality to it that Orlena turned her head and stared at him.

"Not going back?" she managed to gasp in surprise. The thought of not going back had seemed so ridiculous that she had never taken her brother's words seriously, until now. "What do you mean I'm not going back?" She demanded hotly, sitting up swiftly. "Why not?"

"There are several reasons. One is that it is too far away." Norman knew he was not giving the real reason, and he felt half vexed with himself. Must he tell her everything?

"It wouldn't be far away if you moved to the city. You said there were several reasons, what other reasons do you have?"

Should he, dare he tell her the entire reason? He didn't want to, for he was afraid. Not of his sister's temper but of his own. "Always speak the truth, Norman, always!" The words of his uncle Hiram echoed in his mind. Very well, he would tell the truth, but he sent up a swift cry for help from the One who always hears.

"That is one reason, Orlena. Another is the cost. That school is very expensive, not including the train fares to and from town for vacations and holidays. But the biggest reason is that I have seen graduates from that school and . . ." here he paused and drew a breath. "I have no desire to see my sister act or look like one of them." There, the whole truth was out. Norman braced himself for an explosion.

"You would rather see your sister, the granddaughter of one of the most respected families in Blank City, brought up as a country drudge instead of an accomplished young lady?" Orlena's voice had risen to a shout. "I told you, you only cared for yourself! All you want is a slave to do your bidding. Well, I won't be a slave! I won't! I won't!" Springing to her feet, the spoiled, pampered, outraged girl hurled her book across the room at her brother. "Bring down my trunk at once," she screamed, looking wildly around for anything else to throw. "You don't love me! No one loves me!"

Norman crossed the room and grasped his sister's

shoulders. "Orlena!" He gave her a light shake to get her attention, "Stop that screaming," he ordered sternly. "It is because I do love you that I won't let you go back to that school. Now that is enough. You're acting like a baby."

At that Orlena stopped her screaming and stood still at once. "Did you call me a baby?" she demanded furiously.

"No, I simply said you were acting like one." Or like a spoiled brat, he thought to himself.

Twitching away from her brother's hands the irritated girl turned away. "I want to go home," she pouted.

Feeling exasperated by Orlena's constant selfishness, Norman knew he had to end this conversation quickly or he would lose his temper. The room was now quite dark, for the sun had set, and after a hard day of work, the master of Triple Creek Ranch was tired. This did not help any.

Then, into the darkness a light sprang on and a quiet voice spoke. "Aren't you two ever going to stop talking and get to bed?"

Norman and Orlena both looked up startled. There in the doorway stood Jenelle. Her light hair was loose about her shoulders and she smiled. Seeing Norman open his mouth, Jenelle gently shook her head and beckoned to Orlena. "Come dear. You must be tired. Would you like a glass of milk before going to bed?"

Like one in a daze, Orlena nodded and followed her sister-in-law without a word.

Left alone in the room, Norman dropped exhausted into the chair Orlena had vacated and leaned his head wearily on his hand. Would this be life for the next ten years, he wondered? Why was this job of helping Orlena left to him? And Jenelle wasn't feeling well, and they needed rain soon and . . . Norman Mavrich groaned.

"My poor Norman. Why did you try to talk to her now when you were already tired and so was she?" the gentle chiding of Jenelle's voice sounded sweetly at his elbow.

"What are you doing up?" he asked, putting out his hand and drawing his little wife to his knees and ignoring her question. "You should be in bed."

A soft little laugh was the only answer and Jenelle laid her head on her husband's shoulder.

"What did you do with my sister?" he asked at last.

"She's my sister too," his wife quietly reminded him. "I gave her a glass of milk and let her go up to bed. Poor girl, I feel sorry for her, Norman."

"Sorry for Orlena?" And Norman peered down into his wife's face.

"Yes, sorry. She doesn't know what she really wants. She thinks she wants to be in society because she thinks that is what is going to satisfy the longing of her heart."

"What longings does she have besides for fine things and her own way?"

"Didn't you hear her cry?" Jenelle sat up, her face troubled and the tears in her eyes gleaming in the gas light. "She wants love. I heard her from upstairs, Dear. That is what she is missing."

The rancher's face was puzzled. "But Darling," he protested, "she had Grandmother's love. She was given everything she wanted."

"That is just my point. She had a sort of love. No doubt your grandmother thought she was giving her all her love, but true love doesn't give you everything you want, but what you really need. The problem with Orlena is that she doesn't know what true love really is and so when she doesn't get her way, she thinks that love is missing."

"And it doesn't help if I lose my temper with her either," Norman sighed.

Jenelle leaned her head once more on Norman's shoulder and closed her eyes. Her head still ached and she was tired.

After a few minutes Norman spoke quietly. "Let's get up to bed instead of falling asleep here in the chair."

Leaving the light off in her room, Orlena undressed quickly and flung herself onto her bed. Never did she remember being so miserable. Her head ached and her heart ached. She didn't know exactly what she wanted, but she knew she didn't have it. The lump in her throat grew bigger and at last she let the tears come and cried herself to sleep.

When Orlena didn't appear for breakfast the following morning, Norman rose from his seat with a frown.

"Where are you going, Norman?" Jenelle asked, coming into the dining room at that moment.

"To get Orlena. I told her she was to eat breakfast with us now."

Jenelle laid a restraining hand on her husband's arm. "Let me go, Dear. She could just be late as she was Sunday morning."

"I don't want to push my responsibility on to your shoulders," Norman began but Jenelle's soft laugh cut him short.

"You aren't. Didn't you hear me volunteer to go?" Rising to her toes, Jenelle kissed him quickly and slipped from the room. She was feeling much better than she had the night before though when she stopped to notice it, there was still a faint throbbing in her head.

Knocking softly on Orlena's door, Jenelle wasn't surprised to hear no answer. Quietly she opened the door and looked in. Orlena still lay in bed.

"Orlena," Jenelle called, as she gently shook the girl's shoulder.

A moan was the only answer.

Placing her hand on her young sister's forehead, Mrs. Mavrich's face grew troubled. Slipping silently from the room, she returned to her waiting husband in the dining room.

"Well?" Norman asked as she entered. "Is she coming?"

Jenelle shook her head. "I think she's sick. She feels warm and I only got a moan out of her when I tried to wake her."

"Sick?" Norman turned towards the stairs. He couldn't help but wonder if Orlena was pretending to be sick so as to get her own way. However, upon reaching her room, he no longer doubted. The pale face on the pillow, the hot hands and restless movement convinced him.

"I'll have one of the men ride into town for Doctor French," Norman spoke quietly, turning to his wife.

Jenelle nodded.

The doctor pronounced Orlena sick, but not seriously so. She was to remain in bed and he'd be back to check on her that evening.

Mr. and Mrs. Mavrich followed the doctor downstairs and to the front room.

"What is it, Doctor?" inquired Norman, his arm about Jenelle's waist.

"Well, I'd say it could be a combination of many things. Tell me, has she eaten three meals a day regularly?"

"No."

"Has she had any fits of fright or anger?"

"Yes."

"Yep," the doctor nodded his head. "Thought so. Temper, obstinacy and a rather delicate constitution can be a difficult combination. Now I'm not saying," he hastened to add, noticing the looks on Norman and Jenelle's faces. "I'm not saying that her every whim must be satisfied, for a city bred girl like her would sooner eat cake and drink coffee then wholesome bread and milk."

Jenelle couldn't hold back a smile at the doctor's accurate picture of Orlena.

"Now I'll give you a list of what she can and should eat and it'll be up to you to see that she does. Her temper and obstinacy might cause some difficulty in that regard but the Mavrichs aren't known around here for giving up during hard times, eh?"

"I hope not, Doctor," Norman returned the older man's smile and held out his hand. "Thank you for coming by, sir."

"Not at all, not at all, Mr. Mavrich. Now," and he sat down at the desk and wrote rapidly for a minute on a piece of paper before handing it to Jenelle and standing up again. "The list of food for the child. I'll call again this evening, but should she grow worse don't hesitate to call me sooner."

After he was gone, Norman sighed. "Well, I suppose I ought to go and tell Hardrich he's in charge for the day."

"Nonsense!" protested Jenelle. "What would you do if you remained at the house? You would be no help in the kitchen, and I have had more nursing experience than you. I'm afraid you would only worry Orlena by constantly tramping up and down the stairs."

"All right," Norman agreed, reluctantly. "You are right as usual. If you are sure you feel up to it." And Norman looked closely into his wife's face. He didn't like the idea of leaving her at the house with his sister sick, but what she had said was true. "I'll come back or send one of the hands to check on you during the day."

Jenelle agreed to this and handed him his hat. "I'm going up to Orlena," she told him with a smile, "Have a good day, Dear."

The day wore slowly away. Orlena was fretful and cross. She didn't want any chicken broth and the toast was too dry or too soft and all in all acted as the doctor had said. Jenelle kept her voice gentle and sweet and Orlena never guessed just how tired her sister was. The sun continued to blaze and there was no breeze to relieve the heat of summer. As Jenelle sat bathing her young sister's face, she wished she could lie down for a bit, for her own head ached.

Norman sent a message to his wife that afternoon telling her that St. John would cook their supper. That was a relief, for Jenelle had been dreading going back to the hot kitchen. As it was, she didn't feel as though she wanted to eat again.

When the doctor came later, he said Orlena would

come around all right he felt sure, but she should remain in bed for several more days at least. Then he looked sharply at Jenelle. "And what about you? You ought to be in bed yourself."

"It's just the heat, Doctor," Jenelle insisted. "I'll be all right once it cools off a bit."

"Humph," was all the answer the doctor gave before he climbed in his buggy and drove off.

"I wonder if it is just the heat," Jenelle whispered to herself as she slowly mounted the stairs once more. "It has to be. I can't get sick now.

.

T

CHAPTER 12

AN ANSWERED PRAYER

It was later than usual when Norman came back to the house. Jenelle went down to him as soon as she heard his footsteps.

"I thought you had decided to stay out there all night," she told him with a smile.

"Nope." Norman hung up his hat, "Alden, Scott and I were fixing a fence in the back pasture and it took longer than I thought. Didn't St. John or Hearter stop by?"

Slowly Jenelle shook her head. "I don't think so, but they could have come in softly and I didn't hear."

"How's Orlena?"

"Fretful. The doctor said she is no worse."

Mr. and Mrs. Mavrich had mounted the stairs as they talked and entered their room. Noticing the paleness of his wife's face, Norman frowned.

"What is it?" Jenelle asked him, sinking into her rocking chair with a slight sigh.

"You," was the unexpected answer.

"Me?" Blinking in surprise, Jenelle stared in astonishment at Norman's reflection in the mirror.

For a minute only the splashing of water was heard, but when Norman could speak again he replied, "Yes, you. You are pale and look tired. As soon as St. John rings the bell, I'm sending you over to eat. I'll remain here with Orlena until you return. Then I'll go eat."

"Norman—" she began.

"Sweetheart," Norman interrupted her, "have you eaten anything since breakfast?"

Jenelle nodded. It hadn't been much, but it was something. "It's the heat," she began her protest again. "I just don't feel like eating anything." She looked pleadingly at her husband.

Suddenly a rumble of thunder was heard and Norman dashed to the window with Jenelle close behind him. "Look at those storm clouds, Jenelle!" he exclaimed. "Those weren't there when I came home. Thank God! We need rain," he added fervently.

The trees around the house began to sway in the wind, and the curtains, which had hung so still and motionless for so many days, danced on the breeze. Jenelle dropped to her knees before the open window and closed her eyes, letting the refreshing air stir her dress, whip her hair and cool her hot cheeks. Another rumble of thunder sounded, closer this time and Norman, who was watching the sky, saw the fork of lightning in the dark clouds.

The sound of the dinner bell from the bunk house followed the thunder and caused Norman to step back from the window as Jenelle reluctantly rose to her feet.

"Norman," she pleaded. "I don't want to be stuck out in the bunk house when the rain comes. Suppose you go over and bring me a plate of supper and then you can go eat with the men. I'll just eat with Orlena and try to get her to eat some more."

Before he replied, Norman brushed his hand caressingly down Jenelle's face and cupping her small chin in his hand lifted her face. "You're tired," he remarked. "All right," he added. "But you have to promise to eat," and he tried to look stern but failed completely.

"I promise."

Jenelle did eat when Lloyd brought a plate, heaped with

St. John's wonderful cooking, to her, but her appetite was poor and feeling the need to be with Orlena since she was awake, made it more difficult to settle down to an empty kitchen and dining room for a large meal.

Orlena lay silent, watching the brilliant lightning streak across the sky in jagged paths, lighting up the clouds, and listening to the thunder rumble and roll, now in the distance, now close at hand, while the wind, as though trying to make up for the stillness of the past days, bowed the tree tops, lashed the branches and whipped the leaves about; it was a fascinating display and Jenelle, sitting beside Orlena's bed, watched out the windows with her. It was there that Norman found them just as the clouds seemed to split wide open and the rains poured down on the dry, thirsty earth.

"Quite a storm, isn't it?" he remarked in a lull between crashes of thunder.

Jenelle turned. "I was afraid you had gotten caught in the bunk house when it began to rain."

"No, I made it back before it let loose, but I rather think that Hearter and Scott may be stuck in the barn a while unless they don't mind being drenched." He stepped across to a window and tried to look out, but it was only when the lightning flashed that he could see much. "This rain ought to cool things off a bit," he remarked after several minutes, as the thunder lessened and the wind calmed down somewhat.

There was no answer from the other occupants of the room and Norman turned.

Orlena, lulled by the sound of the rain, had fallen asleep and Jenelle had leaned her head on the back of the chair and was staring vacantly at the ceiling.

"Come on," he said, touching his wife's arm, "Orlena shouldn't need you until morning."

It rained all night and the air felt clean and fresh instead of hot, dry and dusty. Jenelle felt more rested than she had in days and, since there were many things that needed to be done, she was grateful for the cooler weather.

The day was a busy one for Mrs. Mavrich. There was laundry to wash, bread to make, rooms to dust, chickens to feed, as well as trying to amuse and nurse Miss Orlena. Jenelle didn't know why, but after ten minutes spent in her sister's room, she felt more tired than after washing a tub full of clothes. "Perhaps," she mused, "it is because I can think when I wash clothes, while in Orlena's room, she scarcely gives one time to think," and Jenelle began kneading her bread. "I wonder if Orlena would enjoy making the beds? Dusting? Taking care of the chickens?" At every chore she shook her head. She couldn't imagine Orlena enjoying any thing that looked like work.

Suddenly she sat down and put a flour covered hand to her head. She felt strangely tired. "Really, Jenelle," she scolded herself. "This is not much more than you normally do. What is wrong with you?" After a few minutes the feeling passed and she went back to work.

The sun came out in the afternoon and the air grew heavy. "I don't know which is worse," Jenelle murmured, wiping her hot face with a damp towel as she prepared supper. "The dry heat and stillness before the storm or this heavy air after the storm. At least there is a breeze."

It was during supper that Norman, after watching Jenelle closely, said abruptly, "You need some one to help you."

Jenelle laughed. "You sound like your sister," she told him. "And what would I do with help? And who would help?"

"Maybe Mrs. Carmond would lend us Flo for a few weeks."

With a smile, Jenelle shook her head. "I'm sure she couldn't. Not with the new baby and Mr. Carmond's invalid mother coming next week. She is the one that needs help."

Norman frowned. "Maybe I'll check some of the other ranches. Surely someone could come."

Again Jenelle shook her head. "Darling, don't you remember that the other ranches have as much work as we do? I'm sure no one could be spared. Please don't worry about me. Orlena will be out of bed in another day or so, the doctor said, and she can help some."

"I have a feeling that she will cause more work instead of helping with it," Norman predicted with a frown.

Inwardly, Jenelle agreed with him, but it wouldn't help matters to say so, therefore, she laughed and rose to clear the dishes away.

In the kitchen such a wave of tiredness swept over her that she leaned against the counter and closed her eyes.

"Jenelle!" Norman had his arms around her before she could open her eyes. "Darling, you aren't well."

"I'm only tired, Norman. Please don't make a fuss," and her blue eyes looked up into his grey ones. "It's been a busy day but—"

"But nothing. You are going to bed."

Jenelle made a feeble protest but the thought of bed was too inviting to really argue. "As soon as I do the dishes," she started.

"I'm washing the dishes tonight. I may not be much of a hand with cooking, but Uncle Hiram made sure I knew about dishes. Now you," he kissed the fair, pale face in his arms, "are marching straight up to bed, or shall I carry you?" he offered.

"I can walk," Jenelle giggled

"There has to be someone who can come help out for a few weeks. At least until Jenelle is rested and Orlena has settled into life here," Norman thought as he washed the dishes. "Jenelle is right, though, every ranch is just as busy as we are. Perhaps there is someone in town who could help . . ." Here a new thought struck him. Did he really want someone from town coming and then spreading stories about his sister? It was hard enough going into town for shopping or church without an added person looking on every day.

"We need one who won't be shocked by Orlena and who won't need to be trained in what needs to be done." Norman spoke aloud in the empty kitchen as he began to wipe the clean dishes and put them away in the cabinets. When the kitchen was spotless, he stepped to the door and looked out as the evening light fell quietly on the barn, corrals and fields.

Looking up into the sky full of soft colors, Norman prayed, "Lord, we need help. You know Jenelle needs a rest but she can't get one unless we have help. It must be just the right help, for wrong help would only add to our difficulties with Orlena. There must be someone who can come help—" Norman blinked as a thought struck him. "That was a quick answer, Lord. Thank you. I'll go right in and write."

It was half an hour later before Norman entered his bedroom. A light was on and quietly he moved over to his dressing table. Pulling out a drawer, he began rummaging through it.

"Norman, aren't you coming to bed?"

Norman turned. Jenelle lay looking at him from her pillow.

"What are you looking for?"

"Just a paper I had. Ah, I have it now." He took up a pen and copied something down. "I will only be gone a minute. I must just take this out to Hardrich."

Jenelle watched him, puzzled. At last she settled down, murmuring, "It was probably something for the ranch."

Several days passed. Jenelle felt rested and refreshed each morning but by mid day was often so tired that she had to sit down and rest for a little while. Orlena continued to improve in health but not in disposition. She was fretful and cross at the slightest thing. Her sister took her sharp words and cutting remarks without a show of irritation, always trying to shield her husband from knowledge of them, for she well knew his indignation and sense of honor would make it harder for him to love his sister as he ought.

As for Norman, he tried to help his wife when he could and often St. John prepared meals for both the ranch house as well as the bunk house.

T

It was four days after Norman had sent Jenelle to bed and washed the dishes himself that he found a letter addressed to him when Lloyd Hearter returned from town. Eagerly he ripped it open and scanned the short note it contained.

"Dear Mr. Mavrich,

It's honored I am that you have thought of me. I have all my affairs taken care of and can stay with you as long as you have need. Have no worries about me, I know what to expect. I will be arriving on Wednesday on the 10:47 train. If you cannot come for me yourself or send one of your men, no doubt I can find someone who will take me out to Triple Creek Ranch . . ."

"Good news, sir?" Hearter asked, for he had been anxiously watching Mr. Mavrich's face and had seen the relieved look which came over it as he read.

"Excellent news, Hearter!" Norman exclaimed. "It's an answered prayer. Where's Hardrich?" He had refolded the letter and replaced it in the envelope which he now tapped on his hand.

"I haven't seen him since I rode in, sir, but I'll check the barn when I take the team in to unhitch them."

Mr. Mavrich nodded and after hesitating a moment, he strode towards the nearby pasture where some of the men were working.

It was there that his foreman found him, and the two men talked for some time. At last Hardrich said, "That would do. What time are you planning to leave?"

"Oh about ten I'd say. But I think I'll remain at the house in the morning and will just hitch up the team myself. There's that new horse that needs worked with. We've been so busy no one has had time."

Hardrich nodded and, after a few more words, Norman moved towards the barn.

"Jenelle," Norman began as the two of them were sitting at the supper table that evening, "I'm going to have to go into town in the morning; is there anything you need me to pick up for you?"

"I don't think so. We picked up supplies not very long ago. Didn't Lloyd just go into town today?" she asked.

Norman nodded.

"Then why do you have to go in tomorrow?" his wife pressed.

"It's just something he couldn't do today," and Norman shrugged. He had thought of mentioning the letter to Jenelle but had second thoughts. "She'd wear herself out trying to get ready," he reasoned and decided to keep it a secret.

The rest of the meal was eaten in silence, for Jenelle was still not her usual self and didn't have the energy to talk much.

The clock in the front room was striking ten when Norman drove out the lane leaving a puzzled wife behind him, for before he left he had come in and put on a clean shirt.

"I do hope he isn't going to town looking for someone to help me," Jenelle sighed, watching the dust settle behind the wagon. "It's not that I wouldn't like a little extra help," she said aloud to the empty front room as she turned from the window. "But I can't think of a single person who could be spared for such work." An imperative voice called her just then and Jenelle gave up trying to understand her husband's errand in town and hurried to Orlena's room.

Orlena was making the most of her sickness. Since she was in bed, she didn't have to sew or do anything else she didn't want to do. Her demands to be amused, have a cold drink brought to her or to be fanned, were endless, and there were times when Jenelle refused to follow her whims. These refusals, always given gently and because Jenelle had other matters to attend to or because some requests went against the doctor's orders, were received with indignation, for Orlena had not learned to accept any way but hers without a fuss.

It was after Mrs. Mavrich had brought a glass of cold water to Orlena for the seventh time that morning, that the sound of wagon wheels was heard in the yard. Stepping to the window, Jenelle looked out, remarking, "Norman has returned and—" then she paused.

"And what?" the demand sounded from the bed.

Jenelle didn't turn her head. "He has someone with him."

"Who?" Orlena persisted.

Jenelle didn't answer but turned swiftly from the window and hurried from the room.

"Jenelle Mavrich!" Orlena called after her. "Don't you dare leave me until you tell me who came!"

The words were wasted for Jenelle was already half way down the stairs. Who had Norman brought? It was a woman, Jenelle had seen that plain enough from the window, but who was she and why was she here? Hurrying to the door, she flung it open and met her husband on the steps.

"Darling," he said, kissing her, "I'd like you to meet Mrs. O'Connor. Mrs. O'Connor, my wife."

CHAPTER 13

RELIEF

"Ah, it's a pleasure at last to meet you," the former housekeeper of Mrs. Marshall Mavrich exclaimed, shaking hands with Jenelle first and smiling warmly.

After returning the greeting, Jenelle turned puzzled eyes on her husband. What was his grandmother's housekeeper doing here?

"Ah, Norman," Mrs. O'Connor chuckled, seeing the unasked questions in Jenelle's eyes. "I see you have not told your sweet wife of my letter."

"I didn't tell her of either letter," Norman chuckled. "I knew if I did, she would work herself sick trying to get ready in the event that you should come. Come now, let us go inside. The heat out here is too much for you ladies." So saying, Norman opened the door and bowed as Jenelle and Mrs. O'Connor entered, then he followed with a small trunk.

"I still don't understand, I'm afraid," Jenelle said, somewhat bewildered and sitting down in the first chair she came to.

"It is a simple matter really," Norman replied. "I realized you were right about no one around here being able to come help. I also knew we needed someone who understood the situation and could help. That is when the Lord brought Mrs. O'Connor to mind. So, I wrote to ask if she would come, and here she is."

Jenelle was evidently not her usual quick self, for she

still stared confusedly at her husband. "But what is she here for?"

"Child," Mrs. O'Connor spoke before Norman had a chance to. "I'm here to do anything you need done. I can clean, cook, tend to Orlena, make beds and wash clothes. I'm not sure but I could feed chickens or gather eggs though never have I done so before."

Jenelle was speechless. The thought of having someone to talk to who wouldn't always be complaining, not to mention the help she would have, was a relief so wonderful that she couldn't say a word for a full minute. Then she laughed. Rising she said with another laugh, "I'm delighted to have you here, Mrs. O'Connor, really. I wasn't expecting help and—" her eyes filled suddenly with tears of joy and relief. Blinking them back she smiled and turned to her husband. "Norman take Mrs. O'Connor's trunk up to the west corner room. I haven't had a chance to dust it today and the bed needs to be aired and—"

Shouldering the trunk, Norman interrupted Jenelle. "See what I mean?" he chuckled to Mrs. O'Connor. "Trying to plan more work already."

Laughing, the ladies followed Norman up the stairs and down the hall. Orlena's voice could be heard calling for Jenelle.

Once they reached the west corner room and Norman had set the trunk down, remarking that he would go unhitch the team, Mrs. O'Connor glanced about her with an approving smile and said, "Now, Mrs. Mavrich, which would you be liking me to do first, see to Miss Orlena or unpack my trunk?"

Jenelle paused in the doorway and spoke somewhat hesitantly, for she was not used to giving orders regarding the house to strangers. "If you wouldn't mind stepping in to see Orlena, it might be pleasant for her to see a familiar face. I could dust your room and air the sheets. But," she added, hearing Orlena's raised voice calling her, "perhaps I should go to Orlena . . ." Without thinking, her hand moved to her aching head at the thought of her fractious young sister.

"No, I'll see to Orlena," Mrs. O'Connor said briskly, noticing the tired look on Jenelle's face. "I am used to her and will settle her quickly and then come back and settle this room. Why don't you sit down and rest, Child?" And Mrs. O'Connor bustled down the hall to answer Orlena's demands.

Left alone, Jenelle gave a sigh and smiled faintly. "I have a feeling Norman brought me an angel. With her to help, perhaps I won't be so tired by the middle of the day." She meant to start dusting the room, but instead sat down for just a moment, in a low rocker, and when Mrs. O'Connor returned some fifteen minutes later she started up in surprise.

"I must have fallen asleep," Jenelle yawned. "I almost never sleep during the day unless I have a sick headache." She started to get up but her new housekeeper waved her back.

"No, Mrs. Mavrich, just sit there and if you feel up to it, we can talk. This room can wait till tomorrow to be dusted and it won't take long to unpack my trunk entirely." She was busy as she spoke, unlocking the trunk and raising the lid. "If those few minutes were enough time for you to sleep in, it is tired you are."

"But I shouldn't be tired," Jenelle protested. "I've hardly done any real work this morning, for Orlena has needed . . ." she paused to consider what it was that Orlena really had needed and ended at last with a soft, "me."

Mrs. O'Connor nodded wisely. "And how often was it that she sent you for a drink this morning when the pitcher of water was beside her bed?"

"Maybe half a dozen times, but the water in the pitcher wasn't as cool as—"

"As Miss Orlena would like," finished Mrs. O'Connor dryly. "I know. I've lived with her most of her life."

Norman remained at the house for the noonday meal, and while they ate he explained that Orlena was not the one giving orders about the ranch and Mrs. O'Connor needn't give in to her every whim.

"Jenelle," Norman turned to his wife, "I saw Dr. French in town this morning and he said he'd be out this evening unless he receives a call elsewhere."

Jenelle nodded. Perhaps the doctor would say that Orlena should get up. Would it be easier then or more difficult to deal with her?

"—Mrs. O'Connor. Won't you, Dear?"

Jenelle turned a blank face to her husband. "Won't I what?" she asked. "I'm afraid I wasn't listening."

"I really should send you to bed," Norman smiled at her. "Or I could have Dr. French look at you."

Jenelle shook her head, returning the smile. "I was only thinking. What did you say?"

"I said you were going to go lie down and rest this afternoon and leave Orlena to Mrs. O'Connor. Won't you?"

Looking astonished, Jenelle shook her head. "Why Norman, Mrs. O'Connor only arrived this morning! I wouldn't dream of pushing Orlena off on her. She should be the one to rest."

A rich chuckle sounded across the table and Mrs. O'Connor spoke, "Ah, Norman, you have a thoughtful wife, indeed. But Deary," and she turned to Jenelle, "I'm not the least bit tired and I imagine a good long rest would do you good. Orlena can tell me all about what has happened since I last saw her and you needn't fret a wee bit about it."

"But—"

"Darling," Norman said gently, placing a hand tenderly on her arm, "please. For my sake, get some rest and don't worry about Orlena or Mrs. O'Connor. Tonight, after the doctor comes, we can have a long talk if you want and plan everything, but this afternoon . . ." His grey eyes were soft and pleading as they gazed into his wife's tired face.

Giving a sigh, Jenelle closed her eyes a moment and then looked up to say with a slight laugh, "I am out numbered, so I'll rest. If," she looked at Mrs. O'Connor, "you are sure you feel up to it."

"She is to get up tomorrow," Dr. French said. "And see that she has something to do besides sit around all day. She's not an invalid." It was evening, and Jenelle and Mrs. O'Connor had followed the doctor down to the front room where Norman was waiting for them. "What that child needs now is some exercise, and you," the doctor wheeled suddenly to Jenelle, "could do with less exercise and more rest."

"That is why Mrs. O'Connor is here, Doctor," Norman answered, putting an arm about his wife. "She'll see to it that Jenelle gets her rest when I'm out on the ranch."

"And that Orlena has things to do?" Doctor French shook his head and picked up his hat. "I hope you are a strong woman, Mrs. O'Connor, for I have a feeling Mr. Mavrich is handing you a full time job."

Mrs. O'Connor smiled, "I'm used to working. A sad thing it would be indeed if Margaret Patrick O'Connor had to sit and rock all the rest of her days. A sad thing entirely!" Now and then a bit of Mrs. O'Connor's Irish upbringing would slip into her speech bringing a smile to Norman's face.

"Good!" was the emphatic reply of the doctor as he slapped on his hat. "Good evening." And Dr. French took his leave.

"I'll just step up to settle Miss Orlena for the night before retiring myself."

"Oh, Mrs. O'Connor," Jenelle protested, starting forward, but Norman held her back. "You've been busy ever since you arrived this morning; I can see to Orlena. You must be tired."

"And me just finished saying I didn't want to be sitting down with folded hands," exclaimed Mrs. O'Connor lifting her hands and looking from Norman to Jenelle.

"Darling," Norman chided softly, his grey eyes laughing, "you wouldn't want Mrs. O'Connor's first night here to be difficult, would you?"

Jenelle turned her face to her husband's with a look of

surprise. "No, but—"

"Then I think it would be best if you let her take care of my sister this evening."

For a moment she looked at him, then turned to look at the ranch's latest addition, and her ready laugh bubbled out though it wasn't as light as usual. "Of course," she agreed. "You must have missed Orlena when Norman took her away. I just can't seem to think for I'm so—"

"Tired," Norman contributed.

Not waiting for anything further to be said, Mrs. O'Connor slipped from the room leaving the master of Triple Creek Ranch alone with his wife.

After the door closed, Norman drew Jenelle over to the sofa and pulled her down beside him. For several minutes neither of them spoke.

"Norman," Jenelle said at last, her head resting comfortably on his shoulder, "what am I to do with Mrs. O'Connor? I don't know how . . . I mean, I've never had anyone old enough to be my mother . . . Well, . . . Oh, Norman, why did you ask her to come?"

There was the sound of tears in Jenelle's voice and Norman looked down at the face half hidden on his shoulder and pulled her closer. "Sweetheart," he whispered, "Mrs. O'Connor was the only real friend I had when I went to visit Grandmother. I knew she didn't have any place to go after the house in town was rented, and you needed help. Darling, she knows what Orlena is like, she knows her moods, her attitudes and her whims. Mrs. O'Connor also knows how to cook and keep house. More important, she knows how to pray. You won't have to tell her much except maybe how to take care of the chickens unless—" He paused in thought, tapped his fingers on his knee and then resumed. "Perhaps it would be good to give the chickens into my sister's care."

Jenelle sat up suddenly, "Norman, she's my chicken too!"

"What?"

"I . . . I mean, my sister," Jenelle giggled, and Norman

laughed.

"All right, Dear, our sister," Norman conceded when his laugh was over.

Jenelle leaned back against his arm. "Norman, if Mrs. O'Connor is in charge of our sister, does the cooking, washing and keeping house, what is left for me? Shall I go out and work in the fields with you and the men? You know I can rope a cow and mend a fence."

"Not a chance." Norman bent his head and kissed the tip of his wife's nose. "You are to do whatever you feel like doing. If you wish to wash the clothes or cook or sew with Orlena, why do so, but if you are tired or feel a sick headache coming on, then you are to go to bed knowing that the house will continue to run smoothly. How does that sound, Sweet?"

"Delightful. But I'm afraid it will take some getting used to." Jenelle sighed softly and nestled in her husband's arms.

The clock on the mantel ticked the minutes slowly by, the only sound in the room, until Mr. and Mrs. Mavrich rose to kneel beside the sofa and spend some time in prayer.

That night Norman lay awake for some time listening to Jenelle's soft, even breathing beside him and staring into the dark, thinking. He knew Mrs. O'Connor would be a wonderful help to Jenelle and would settle in to the ways of the house easily, but he wasn't so sure about Orlena's actions. "I'm never sure how my young sister will act," he sighed to himself. "She is puzzling and difficult." Should he leave the adjusting and settling of everything, Jenelle, Mrs. O'Connor, Orlena and the work, to settle itself somehow, or should he try to help? Would he only add to the confusion he felt sure Orlena would cause if he tried to help? It would be easier for him if he let things work themselves out. "But perhaps I should stay," he mused. "I might help Jenelle if I stayed here, but what about the work on the ranch?"

He smiled in the dark at his own thinking. If Hardrich couldn't run the ranch for a few days without Norman in the fields too, he would have to change a lot since he saw him a few hours ago. "I'll stay here at least tomorrow and see how things go," he decided. Then he turned over, closed his eyes and fell asleep.

"Come, Miss Orlena." Mrs. O'Connor entered the room to find Orlena awake. "The doctor said you were to be getting up this morning and breakfast will be ready in ten minutes." She had bustled about as she spoke and opened the curtains so that the light of the early morning would enter.

"Oh, I can't get up this morning, Mrs. O'Connor," Orlena objected, trying to look pitiful. "Perhaps by this afternoon I'll have enough strength to get up for a time. I'll sleep a little longer and then you or Jenelle can bring my breakfast."

"We'll do no such thing." Mrs. O'Connor turned to the bed and pulled the sheet off.

"How dare you!" exclaimed Orlena, bouncing upright and glaring, seeming to forget in her anger that she was "still weak and sickly."

"The sheet needs washing. Your clothes are on the chair. You'd best be putting them on, for Norman and Jenelle will be waiting for us."

"Us?" Orlena repeated. "I will eat in the dining room, and you will eat in the kitchen. I refuse to eat with hired help."

"You won't be eating anywhere unless you get dressed," Mrs. O'Connor replied calmly.

Orlena moved over to the chair. "You'll have to help me get dressed, Mrs. O'Connor, or I'll never be ready in time and then Norman will be angry at me." She whimpered like a child afraid of his own shadow, but Mrs. O'Connor wasn't deceived.

"What you need, Child, is some sensible clothes you can dress yourself in without keeping your brother waiting."

The dress was soon on and Orlena sat down before her mirror and held out her brush to Mrs. O'Connor. "Now fix my hair," she ordered. "Remember, I should have fourteen curls."

But Mrs. O'Connor was not going to cater to the young tyrant any longer. "Tis not likely I'll be doing your hair for ye," she exclaimed, letting her Irish tongue speak with it's old lilt. "I didn't come to play nurse maid to ye when yer old enough to be doin' it yerself. Tis time I was down helpin' Mrs. Mavrich with the breakfast entirely!" And without so much as a by your leave, Mrs. O'Connor disappeared from the room.

CHAPTER 14

UNEXPECTED TEARS

"How . . . how . . . how dare you!" Orlena spluttered. "Mrs. O'Connor!" she hollered. "You come back here this minute. Do you hear me?" She flung open her door and shouted as she had never done even in her grandmother's house. There she would have rung for another servant and then, when her grandmother was present, she would have pouted, whined, complained or cried until the one who had displeased her had been properly punished. "Mrs. O'Connor!" Never had the housekeeper dared to ignore her wishes before. She would speak to Norman about her.

Leaning over the railing, staring down the stairs, Orlena was about to shout again when the door below opened and her brother appeared.

"Good morning, Orlena," Norman looked up to greet her pleasantly.

For a brief moment, Orlena remained standing and stared down. Then she remembered what she was going to tell him and ordered, "Send Mrs. O'Connor to my room at once!"

Norman's eyebrows raised. "That wasn't exactly a pleasant morning greeting," he remarked, adding, "Mrs. O'Connor is busy helping Jenelle get breakfast on the table and I'm afraid can't come now. Is there anything I can do?"

Orlena glared down at him. "No!" she snapped and

started to storm back to her room.

"Breakfast will be in five minutes, Orlena," Norman called after her.

The sound of her door slamming was her only reply.

"Hmm," Norman scratched his head. "I wonder if she will come down this morning for breakfast? She certainly isn't still sick in bed." Shaking his head, he returned to the dining room to stand by the window and drum his fingers on the sill. "This could be an interesting day," he mused.

And so the day started. Orlena did come down for breakfast with a hurt look on her face and complained to her brother in a teary voice about Mrs. O'Connor's rudeness.

His only response was, "We don't always get things our own way. Pass the butter, please, Orlena."

Orlena passed it, muttering under her breath.

To Jenelle's surprise Norman remained about the house all day. Not always inside, but being only out in the barn or in one of the outbuildings, he was often stepping inside for something. As for Mrs. O'Connor, Jenelle's worries about her fitting in were wasted, for before the day was over Mrs. O'Connor felt like one of the family.

"She fits in better than Orlena has yet," Jenelle sighed to herself as she latched the chicken coop and prepared to follow her new housekeeper and Orlena back to the house.

Norman, coming from the barn, fell into step beside his wife. "Have you explained the care of the chickens to Mrs. O'Connor and Orlena?"

Jenelle nodded.

"Good. Orlena," he called, lengthening his stride a bit to catch up with his sister, "starting tomorrow the care of the chickens will be your responsibility."

Stopping short and wheeling around, Orlena stared at her brother. Surely he was joking! He didn't really think that the granddaughter of Mrs. Marshall Mavrich would take care of *chickens*, did he? One look at his face, however, told her that he was not teasing. "I have nothing suitable to wear for such a despicable job," she told him haughtily.

If Orlena thought her lack of proper clothing would deter her brother and make him change his mind, she was sadly mistaken.

"I suppose you'll just have to work harder on sewing your new dresses. Jenelle's dresses don't seem to have suffered from the care of the chickens." Norman glanced critically at his wife's dark blue dress. "Perhaps if you asked politely, Mrs. O'Connor or Jenelle would help you with the sewing. But, the chickens are now your responsibility and," he added firmly in low tones, "I don't want to hear of Jenelle having to take care of them because you forgot. Is that understood?"

His sister's only answer was a glare. She was learning that an argument with her brother didn't usually get her what she wanted.

℘

The next few days were trying ones. More than once Mrs. Mavrich thanked God for her new help and sighed over the problem of her young sister. Orlena, not used to working, not even on such simple things as making her bed and hanging up her clothes, seemed determined to make life as miserable as she could for herself and those around her. She hated the chickens and, on her second day of gathering the eggs, when a hen pecked her hand drawing blood, she shrieked and flung the entire basket of eggs she had already gathered, out the door of the hen house. Of course every egg was smashed and it took some time before the chickens were calm enough to return to eating. Jenelle would have gathered the rest of the eggs that morning had not a grim-faced Mrs. O'Connor marched a furious Orlena back outside to finish the job.

"If she had been a brother instead of a sister—"

Norman growled when he learned of it.

"I know," Jenelle tried to smile. "You would have taken a trip to the woodshed a long time ago."

Not only did Orlena object to the chickens but also to every other chore she was given. She did more complaining, pouting and criticizing than sewing and, had not Jenelle had wonderful patience, all progress on the new clothes would have halted.

Previously, Jenelle had regularly slipped into Orlena's room to straighten it up and make her bed; however, after a talk with Mrs. O'Connor, Jenelle carefully avoided Orlena's room. She knew that if she were to enter it, she wouldn't be able to leave without tidying up. Only Mrs. O'Connor and Orlena knew what state that room was in, until one morning nearly two weeks after the housekeeper's arrival.

Jenelle was in the dining room setting a pitcher of milk on the table when Orlena flung herself into the room.

"Jenelle Mavrich!" she shouted, "You lazy, irresponsible, good for nothing, sister-in-law! How dare you treat me this way!"

Opening her eyes in astonishment at the sudden outburst, Jenelle turned to the irate child. Her first thought was, "I hope Norman is still out in the barn," then aloud she questioned, "What are you talking about, Orlena?"

"Don't try to sound so innocent," Orlena fumed. "You know very well what is wrong. Just look at this dress!"

Jenelle blinked and gazed with puzzled eyes at the lovely black dress. She didn't see anything wrong with it besides some wrinkles, except for it being completely out of place on the ranch. With a shake of her head, Jenelle said patiently, "I still don't know what is wrong. What is it about the dress that you want me to notice?"

Her quiet voice irritated Orlena still further. "The wrinkles, you dumb person! You—"

"Orlena Mavrich, what is it you are calling your sweet sister?" Mrs. O'Connor had entered the room and now stood with her hands on her hips and a frown on her face.

Whirling on this new person, Orlena gave her a scathing look before retorting with fury, "You are just as dumb as my 'sweet sister' as you call her. You are both dumb, selfish, ignorant beasts! It's your fault that I haven't a decent thing to wear."

"What is wrong with the one you are wearing now," ventured Jenelle.

"Wrong with it!" Orlena's voice rose with a shriek. "Wrong with it? It's wrinkled! I already told you!"

"If you would pick up your clothes and hang them up instead of leaving them lying around in heaps, they would not be wrinkled." This calm fact from Mrs. O'Connor was spoken in a normal tone of voice.

"*I* leave them? That is not my job. I am a guest and I consider myself insulted!"

What was she to say to such a child, Jenelle wondered as Orlena's voice continued. How do I stop her before Norman comes in? She sent up a swift, silent prayer for help and wisdom and then said softly, "Orlena, on this ranch, everyone picks up after themselves."

"Well, I don't! You are just a mean, selfish, horrid, ill-bred—"

"Orlena Mavrich! That is enough!"

Instant silence flooded the room. Jenelle quaked inwardly, for she had never heard her husband speak in such a stern, furiously cold voice. The silence went on. No one dared speak. Stealing a quick glance at her husband, she saw his eyes locked with Orlena's and noticed his clenched jaw. Oh, was there nothing she could do? Suddenly she felt as though she couldn't breathe and gripping the table she sank onto a chair gasping for air.

"Darling!" Norman was beside her in an instant. "I'll carry you to your bed," he offered, preparing to lift her.

But Jenelle shook her head and pushed his arm away. "I'm all right, really. I just . . . Oh Norman, what can I do?" And the mistress of Triple Creek Ranch buried her face in her hands and burst into tears.

For several long minutes Orlena just stood and stared. Never had she seen a grown person cry like that. And to think that Jenelle, of all people— She didn't know what to think. Slowly, without a word, she turned around, moved past Mrs. O'Connor and made her way back to her own room. Was she the cause of Jenelle's misery? Did Jenelle really like her a little, even though she herself had never liked Jenelle? Sitting in her chair near the open window, Orlena came face to face with the possibility that most of the misery she had experienced since coming to the ranch was her own fault. She hadn't even tried to like it. All she had done, she realized, was compare this life with the one she had always known. Could she come to like living out in the middle of nowhere if she tried hard enough? Orlena wasn't sure she really wanted to like it at Triple Creek, but— "At least I can tolerate it until time for school," she thought with a deep sigh.

Downstairs Norman was on his knees beside Jenelle. "Darling, please stop crying," he begged, drawing her into his arms. "It wasn't your fault. You didn't do anything. Sweetheart!" He kissed her, smoothed back her hair and then glanced about the room. It was empty except for the two of them. For several minutes he continued talking softly until Jenelle had calmed down enough to listen. "I'm going to have a talk, a calm one, with Orlena."

Jenelle put in a protest. "Don't, Norman, I—"

Gently Norman put his finger over his wife's lips. "I think it is time I did. I won't have you spoken to like that." Then before Jenelle could say anything else, Norman changed the subject. "Has Mrs. O'Connor been a help to you, Sweet?"

"Oh, yes."

"I'm thankful to hear it. Now," he kissed her once again and stood up, "you are going to eat something and then go up to bed."

With a tired sigh, Jenelle leaned against him and clung to his hand. He was so strong and thoughtful, so wise; he always was thinking of her and the ranch. How did she get the most wonderful husband in the world, she wondered?

"Jenelle?"

"I'm not hungry," she whispered, closing her eyes. The dining room was warm, and she was tired.

After helping his wife up to bed, Norman returned to the dining room to find Mrs. O'Connor. As they sat together eating their cold breakfast, Norman recalled the many mornings he had taken his breakfast in the kitchen at his grandmother's with Mrs. O'Connor. And as then, he needed to talk.

"Mrs. O'Connor, what am I supposed to do? I can't talk to Orlena without one of us losing our temper, usually both of us. I can't find out from Jenelle what's been going on in the house, so how can I know what needs to be said? I don't even have the faintest idea what Orlena was so upset about this morning. It's almost as though Jenelle were trying to protect Orlena. Am I that harsh?"

Setting down her tea cup, Mrs. O'Connor shook her head. "Ah Norman," she said, "tis a sweet wife you have. She's not protecting Orlena, she's trying to protect you."

"Me? From what?"

"From yourself."

For a moment Norman puzzled over that statement. How could Jenelle be trying to protect him from himself and why did she think she should? He must be missing something, but what?

"And here I was thinking you had a fine head on your shoulders since you went to college and graduated with such high honors." The housekeeper chuckled over the perplexed look on the rancher's face. "Tis from yer temper she's protecting you. She knows how jealous you are for her and that Miss Orlena has a way of saying things that rile yer temper but have no effect on Jenelle. Her patience is great, though I'll admit this morning was a wee bit too much."

"I'll say it was too much," Norman muttered. Then, with a long, drawn out sigh that was almost like a groan, he began drumming his fingers on the table. Turning suddenly to Mrs. O'Connor, he asked, "Do you think I should talk to Orlena now?"

Thoughtfully the housekeeper shook her head. "Not yet. Wait a bit. I believe Jenelle's tears did more to soften her heart than any words you could say. Go to your work on the ranch."

"But Jenelle . . ."

"I'll see to it that she rests."

After Norman departed reluctantly, Mrs. O'Connor stepped up to Orlena's room. "'Tis not right she should be left hungry entirely," she thought as she tapped softly. A subdued voice answered and Mrs. O'Connor opened the door.

Orlena turned from the closet, her young face sober, her manner hesitant. "I'm not hungry, Mrs. O'Connor. Please don't make me eat. I couldn't swallow anything."

"'Tis a state of things to be sure," the good woman murmured to herself as she descended the stairs to clear away the breakfast that was only half eaten. "And it's unsure I am if tis a good state of things or not."

It was indeed, as Mrs. O'Connor put it, a state of things. Orlena hung up her dresses and took care of the chickens in a subdued manner. Even sewing on her dresses, which were nearly finished, was a silent time, for Orlena didn't complain as she usually did; in fact, she scarcely said two words. Jenelle came down later in the morning, also quiet though not in the same way her young sister was. Several times during the day, Mrs. O'Connor would glance first at Jenelle and then at Orlena. Neither one was moody, Jenelle even smiled, though there was not as much brightness in it as there had been only the day before.

This state of things lasted for several days before Jenelle was once again her bright, sunny self with a cheerful smile and a kind word for everyone. Orlena accepted, at least for the time, her life at Triple Creek and resigned herself to at least tolerating her assigned chores and eating with Mrs. O'Connor. As for eating with the hired hands, Orlena's lip still curled, and she longed for the day when she could put Lloyd Hearter in his place.

T

The fierce heat of the summer had abated and the nights now held a bit of coolness, a hint of the approaching autumn; while during the bright sunny days there was often a cloud or a breeze which offered just a hint of chill, a tantalizing, invigorating, refreshing tang of air to quicken the blood, lighten the eyes and put a new spring in the step. The season was beginning to change and those on Triple Creek Ranch, hired hands, those living in the house and the animals in the barn or pasture, felt a new lease on life. Some days were rainy, but when the sun shone again, not to bake the ground and suck any moisture from the earth, but to change the dry, brown grasses into bright green pastures where the cattle and horses ate with delight, then indeed did the ranch seem alive with life.

The change was enjoyed by all and Jenelle, feeling more refreshed than she had for weeks, went about the house or worked in her gardens among the flowers with a song on her lips and the ever ready smile or bubbling laugh for those she saw.

Orlena, having never experienced the changing of seasons away from the noise, bustle and hurry of the city, found herself almost skipping down the stairs each morning, eager to be finished with her chores so that she might enjoy the day with a book in some secluded place where she would be undisturbed. True, her work often suffered from being sloppily and hastily done; the dusting, which Orlena despised, would often be neglected for days until Mrs. O'Connor or Jenelle spoke to her about it. But once, when her neglect of the chickens had taken Jenelle out to feed them and gather the eggs herself and Norman had discovered it, Orlena had been made to clean out the hen house while her brother stood sternly by watching her. Though she had complained and cried, her brother had remained unmovable until the job had been finished. Ever since that time, Orlena had taken care that whatever other chores might be neglected or hurried over, the chickens never were.

As for Mrs. O'Connor, that good woman relapsed more often into her native tongue and the bright lilt of her Irish melodies danced across the yards while she hung up the wash. "For," she remarked to Hardrich one evening after the Monday night feast, "Tis like a bit 'o the old country entirely. Tis green and bonny. I'm a thinkin' ye can't know how I've missed the grasses growin' entirely."

Hardrich nodded. "I lived in a city two years, and I never will go back if I can help it." He shook his head decidedly and strolled away from the house with the rest of the hands.

Seated alone in her room, watching from behind the plain muslin curtains, Orlena frowned. "Wouldn't go back to the city. What wouldn't I do to go back!" Turning pensively away, she sat down in her chair and thought. Autumn was rapidly approaching and school would be starting soon. Where would she go? She only had a dim hope that Norman would relent and send her to Madam Viscount's Seminary, but if he didn't, where was she to go? "I'll ask him tomorrow at breakfast," she decided and began to undress for bed.

CHAPTER 15

A REFRESHING INTERLUDE

In another room, some time later, the master of the ranch turned from the open window to his wife who was busily brushing out her long, golden hair. "Jenelle," he said, "we have to decide where."

"True," Jenelle agreed quietly. "I've been praying about it."

"So have I," Norman put in. "But the decision has to be made now. I don't feel right about putting it off any longer."

Laying the hairbrush back on her dressing table, Jenelle moved softly over to her husband who had turned back to the window, a worried expression on his face. "Why not here," she whispered, slipping an arm through his and leaning her head on him.

Norman looked down. "You mean in town?"

Jenelle nodded.

For a moment all was silent. "It would be simple," he at last replied slowly. "But not Sheldon's?"

"No. Not yet. Let's wait a while for that. Perhaps next year would do."

Bending his head, Norman dropped a kiss on his wife's bright hair before slipping his arm about her. Silently, together, they stood watching the last of the evening light fade from the sky and the stars come out one by one to twinkle brightly now that the king of day had gone to bed.

It was the following morning, one bright and fresh from a dew that had fallen during the night, and the air which blew the curtains was slightly chilly. The family was seated at the breakfast table when Orlena, turning to her brother, asked in the patronizing voice she had begun using, "Norman, have you yet made up your mind about which academy I am to attend this school term? I do wish you would hurry and decide for I must have time to order my school uniforms and my books and get my trunk packed."

Setting his coffee cup down and exchanging a quick glance with Jenelle, Norman smiled at his sister. "I have decided. Jenelle and I talked it over last night."

"And?" In spite of herself, Orlena was curious about this place where she would be spending the school year. Wherever it was, it would be better than staying out in the middle of nowhere on the ranch she decided.

"You'll be attending school in town this term so you won't need any uniforms. As for books," he went on, not noticing Orlena's surprise and growing anger. "You and Jenelle can go into town with me tomorrow, and we'll find out what you'll need."

"School? In town?" Orlena's voice was full of shocked disbelief. "And where will I be living?"

"Here at the ranch. You can either walk into town, learn to ride a horse, or some days you can no doubt go into town with me or with one of the hands."

Slamming her fork down on the table, Orlena glared at her brother. "I won't walk to town and I won't ride with any old hired hand." Then, with a sudden change of tactics her face grew sober and her eyes filled with tears. "I think you are cruel, Norman," she sniffed, dabbing at her eyes in a way that recalled their first meeting in town. "Cruel. You must not love me at all."

Sighing, Norman frowned and looked annoyed. Why did his sister have to make things so difficult? True, she had done better for a while, but now this! "Orlena, stop. If I didn't love you, would I keep you around here?"

Only a sniff came from behind the napkin where Orlena sat.

Norman opened his mouth to speak, but before any sound came from his lips, Jenelle's gentle hand was placed on his arm. Glancing over at her, he saw a slight shake of her light head. Maybe Jenelle was right. Maybe it would be wiser not to say anything. A quick look at Mrs. O'Connor and Norman returned to his eating.

The silence in the room, except for the sound of eating, lasted so long that at last Orlena let the napkin drop from before her face. To her astonishment and confusion no one looked as though anything had happened. She felt annoyed that no attention had been given to her, but, feeling the pangs of hunger, for she had eaten nothing since noon the day before, she resumed eating.

Draining the last of his coffee, Norman stood up. "Well, I must be off. Work awaits me. Breakfast was perfect. Don't work too hard today and tire yourself out before tomorrow, Darling," Norman said as he stooped to kiss his wife good bye. Then, picking up his hat, he stepped through the door into the bright, beautiful morning.

Jenelle's eyes followed the tall, sturdy figure striding away with such purpose and suddenly longed to be out there with him. Many times before she had helped with ranch work, either on Triple Creek or when she was younger, at her home with her father and brothers. She rode well and could even rope cattle and had helped with the branding in the spring. Turning quickly to Mrs. O'Connor, Jenelle began half hesitatingly, "Would it be imposing if I did not help with washing the dishes?"

"Of course not, Dear. If Orlena and I can't wash and dry these dishes, we're not worth our salt. What are you wanting to be doing?"

"I want to go outside!"

Mrs. O'Connor looked perplexed. "But you're outside

nearly everyday in your gardens."

"I don't want to work in the gardens. I want to go out in the fields, to wander away from the house and barns, to watch the men working and lend a hand too. Oh, I can help," she added as she saw Mrs. O'Connor's smile. "I can drive a nail as straight as anyone, rope a cow, mend a fence and . . . whatever needs to be done. I—"

Interrupting, Mrs. O'Connor waved her hand with dismissal, "Then go, Child. Be off with you. Orlena and I banish you from the house for at least the morning. We don't need you around today, do we, Orlena?"

During this exchange, Orlena had been a silent but interested listener. In her mind Jenelle was too small and petite to do much ranch work besides take care of the house. She couldn't imagine her swinging a hammer, nor could she picture her riding a horse or roping a cow. The idea seemed so impossible that she smiled and agreed with Mrs. O'Connor.

"Oh you are both darlings!" And Jenelle sprang up to run around the table and drop a kiss on the cheek of each one before snatching up the other hat which hung near the place Norman always kept his and dashing from the house.

She was free! Free! Such a glorious, lighthearted, almost girlish feeling swept over Jenelle that she tilted her head back and whistled to the meadowlark flying overhead. Lifting her skirts she gave a little skip of delight and then hurried on. Not once did she look back, so she never knew that in the doorway of the house, two pairs of eyes watched her.

Catching sight of Norman up ahead she called out, "Norman, wait a moment."

He turned in surprise. Jenelle? Surely something must be wrong! Quickly he started to retrace his steps. "Jenelle, what is it? What has happened? What's wrong?"

"Nothing," she retorted, laughing and tossing back her light hair.

"Why are you out here? What happened at the house?" Taking hold of his wife's arms gently, he looked anxiously into her face. "What happened?" he repeated.

Lifting laughing blue eyes up to his worried grey ones, Jenelle reassured him. "Really, nothing has happened except that I was sent away from the house. Banished, just like that," and she snapped her fingers. As her husband started to frown, Jenelle placed her small hands on his shoulders. "I had to get away, Norman. I just had to. Everything was calling me, the horses, the pastures, even the fences seemed to be begging me to come. I couldn't stay at the house any longer. Why I haven't been out here since . . ." she paused a moment in thought. "Norman," she gasped in surprise, "I don't believe I've been out to the fields since the letter came with the news of your grandmother."

"You're sure you want to come with me?"

Jenelle nodded.

"I'll only have Lloyd and Alden with me today. Hardrich has the rest."

"Norman," Jenelle chided with a smile. "I didn't come to see the hands."

Norman grinned. Though he might not have admitted it, there had been days when he had missed the quick, deft way Jenelle had of twisting the wire fences together, her sure and steady hand with a hammer or her calm, soothing way with the horses. Not to mention her light, cheerful talk which kept everyone in fine spirits. Now, with Jenelle at his side, her small, capable hand tucked in his arm, Norman set off again.

"We won't be riding today," he told her. "We're only going to the North Creek pasture."

"The North Creek pasture," Jenelle repeated softly. "That is where we discovered the nest of quail last spring, wasn't it?"

"And you took some of the hands and built a small fence around it before we turned the horses into the field. I remember."

Following a slight trail, Mr. and Mrs. Mavrich climbed a sloping hill, descended the other side and crossed a small flat field before reaching the gate to the North Creek pasture.

Here they discovered Lloyd and Alden already there.

They greeted the mistress of the ranch with delight and then the four of them began work on the fence line. Some new posts were needed to replace rotting ones while here and there a new string of wire was added. Jenelle, though she assisted the men quite a bit, often wandered off to look at a flower, watch a bird or just enjoy the beautiful day. No one complained and often Norman watched her with a bright smile.

"Mr. Mavrich?" Lloyd asked when Jenelle had wandered quite away from the men. "Are things goin' better up at the house these days?"

Norman nodded. "Yes, Hearter, they're better. But please, don't stop praying."

"No sir," Alden put in. "But I'm glad the missus is feeling better though she always seemed all right when I saw her."

No one spoke again for several minutes as they worked on digging a hole for a new fence post. The sun was nearing mid-day and it was quite warm. Norman pulled out his handkerchief and mopped his hot face.

"What say we take lunch in the shade by the creek?"

"No complaints from me, Boss," Lloyd grinned, taking his hat off and wiping his sleeve across his face.

A few minutes later Jenelle joined them and together they settled themselves in the shade of an old tree growing near the edge of North Creek. The lunch St. John had packed was soon nearly gone and only Lloyd was left eating.

"Lloyd," Jenelle turned to the young hand. "Do you know who is teaching school this term?"

Having a family living in town, Lloyd often visited them when he had some spare time and heard the latest news which he would pass on to anyone interested. Nodding, Lloyd swallowed his last bite of cold chicken before replying. "Sure do. Connie's teaching this year."

"Your sister?"

"Yes Ma'am. She got her teachin' certificate in the

spring an' not wantin' to go far to teach, she applied in town an' got the position. Ma said the school board voted the day before I was in town last."

"Oh I'm so thankful!" Jenelle clasped her hands together and her eyes sparkled with delight. "You see, Orlena is going to be attending the school in town this year and it will be so much easier for her if the teacher isn't a complete stranger. Since she's your sister, I'm sure Orlena will feel more at ease."

A quick glance was exchanged between young Hearter and Mr. Mavrich before Lloyd replied somewhat hesitantly, "Mrs. Mavrich, Orlena doesn't like me . . ." his voice trailed away and he looked down.

With a smile, Jenelle laid a gentle hand on his arm, "That was a long time ago, Lloyd," she spoke earnestly. "I'm sure Orlena has forgotten all about it. Now you men had better get back to work and I'll pack these things up."

It wasn't until they were out of earshot that Alden spoke. "Mrs. Mavrich always believes the best of people. I'm afraid I don't do that."

"Me either," Lloyd put in. "I'm ashamed to admit it, but I don't trust people like she does."

"My wife is a rare woman, men." Norman's voice was quiet. "The Good Lord gave me a treasure I don't deserve."

Though neither one said anything, both Hearter and Alden disagreed with Mr. Mavrich. In their eyes Norman Mavrich was a man to be admired and looked up to; his judgment deferred to, his ways unquestioned and his advice followed in every way possible. If Norman got a little hot under the collar at times, it was only for good reason. As for Jenelle, in the eyes of the men, especially Lloyd, Alden, St. John and Hardrich, she could do no wrong. To them and the rest of the hired hands on Triple Creek Ranch, Mr. and Mrs. Mavrich were a perfect match for each other and life on the ranch was all that they could desire.

It wasn't until evening that the master and mistress of

the ranch headed home hand in hand. Both were tired and hungry, but content. It had been a pleasant day out in the fields and Jenelle gave a small sigh of satisfaction. Life seemed to be going smoothly now and tomorrow they would register Orlena for school which would start in a few weeks. If Connie Hearter was teaching, all would be well.

Norman, hearing the sigh asked softly, "Are you tired?"

"Only pleasantly so. I enjoyed being out with you." Her eyes met his and she returned the kiss he gave her.

Behind them, Lloyd and Alden grinned. "You weren't here when he was courtin' her," Alden whispered with a knowing smile.

Jenelle turned then and bade them a merry good-night as they turned off to the bunk house.

"Good night, Mrs. Mavrich, Mr. Mavrich."

Norman glanced back, "Good night, men. See you in the morning."

CHAPTER 16

THE WRONG SHOES

"We'll be leaving in a few minutes, Orlena," Mrs. Mavrich called up the stairs.

A movement was heard and then Orlena's face looked over the railing above. "I've decided I don't want to go in to town this morning. I suppose you can register me without my presence? Good. Then just pick up the books I'll need and if I can't persuade my brother to change his mind about where I'm to go, then when school starts I shall make my way there. Though," she added with an elaborate sigh, "I doubt I'll be able to learn anything. After all, Madam Viscount's Seminary was quite advanced, you know."

"Don't you want to meet your new teacher?" Jenelle had always dreaded meeting new teachers on the first day of school. In her mind meeting them before school had commenced was preferable.

"No, thank you. It matters not the slightest who they are. I know I'll be tired of them long before school is ended so why should I add to the days by meeting them earlier?"

To this Jenelle had no reply and left to join her husband in the light wagon. To his inquiry, she repeated Orlena's reason and shook her head. "I don't think I understand her, Norman. Sometimes she acts like a princess, while other times it's as though nothing matters, yet in it all I often catch glimpses of a longing."

Norman glanced beside him. "What sort of longing?"

"I'm not sure of all of them, but I know she wants to be loved, accepted and," here she paused and a slight smile twitched the corners of her mouth.

"And what?"

"And she wants to be treated as one with Mavrich blood should rightfully be treated."

At that they both laughed. It had often amused Jenelle when Orlena would declare with dignity that she was a Mavrich. She seemed to forget that Norman was and always would be a Mavrich while she would no doubt get married and take on a new name.

"But seriously, Norman," Jenelle continued after the laugh was over, "she puzzles me. I almost feel as though I don't know her even yet."

Reaching out, Norman placed his hand over the small ones clasped in his wife's lap. "Jenelle, I still feel that way after all these years. I never have understood her, and sometimes I wonder if I ever will."

The soft thud of the horse's hooves, the rattle of the wagon over some stones and the cry of an eagle soaring high overhead were the only sounds to be heard for some minutes. Then, in a quiet voice, Jenelle said, "But we'll keep praying for her."

$$T$$

Orlena wasn't able to persuade Norman to change his mind about her school, so on the first day of the new term, she dressed with elaborate care, ignoring the new school dress Jenelle had sewn for her and swept down to the breakfast table looking, as Norman put it later, like a frilly china doll.

"At least she doesn't have on her mourning dress with the train, plaiting, ribbons and lace," Jenelle remarked to Mrs. O'Connor as together they watched the wagon drive away towards town with Norman and Miss Orlena Mavrich. "That dress wouldn't have survived the day I'm sure. Not that the other children would have ruined it purposefully, but . . ."

Mrs. O'Connor nodded. "As it is, she could almost pass for the teacher, if it weren't for the fact that she still looks like a girl."

Turning from the window where the last sign of the wagon and its occupants had disappeared over the hill, Jenelle remarked, "I wonder how her first day of school will go?"

She was to wonder that many times during the day. Norman had come home and said that Orlena had insisted that he leave her before they reached the school. And no, she did not wish him to walk with her. She was not a baby. So Jenelle wondered and waited.

"I believe this is worse than sending my own child off to school," she sighed over her mending and gazed out the window at the empty road. "Then you would know what the child might do and how he would respond, but with Orlena there is no telling what she'll do or say or even how she'll act. Poor Miss Hearter, I do hope she can handle everything."

Mrs. Mavrich need not have worried about Miss Hearter; she was quite capable of taking complete charge of a school room full of children.

As for Orlena, that young lady of importance, for so she viewed herself, quite overawed most of her classmates with her fine clothes and regal air. She had walked into school with her head high and an expression of condescension on her face. "Miss Hearter," she said with cool dignity, "I don't know where you can place me for I have been a student at a large and advanced seminary. It is only because of my grandmother's recent death and the neglect of her lawyer and my brother in securing my place at the seminary this term that I am here. I'm sure I won't be here many weeks before everything will be settled at Madam Viscount's and I will trouble you no longer."

Miss Hearter smiled kindly. She had had a talk with Mrs. Mavrich and knew of no such plans as Orlena put forth. However, she merely said, "We're glad to have you, Orlena, please take a seat so that we may begin."

Finding an empty seat, Orlena made her way there, her skirt rustling as she walked. She had expected to parade her knowledge, but had not been given a chance. Sitting down carefully so as to wrinkle her silk dress as little as possible, she set her books on the desk before her and folded her hands in her lap. Silence filled the room for a moment and then Miss Hearter introduced herself, gave a short welcome, and school was begun.

It was beginning to grow late when Jenelle hurried out to meet the men coming home from the fields. "Norman!" she called before she had reached them.

Norman quickened his pace. He could tell by his wife's voice that something was wrong. But before he could ask, Jenelle, breathless and with a worried expression, told him.

"Orlena hasn't come home from school. Are you sure she knows the way? What could be taking her so long? Do you think she's hurt? Surely she couldn't have been kept after school, not on the first day!"

"She's not home yet?" Norman's face grew grave, and he glanced up at the sun. She should have been home over an hour ago. "I'll saddle up and go look for her. Perhaps she went home with a schoolmate."

Just then Mrs. O'Connor called, "She's home now. No need to go looking." And Mr. and Mrs. Mavrich hurried into the house.

There at the table in the dining room sat a very cross Orlena. "Why didn't someone pick me up after school?" she demanded.

"You told me you would walk home," Norman replied somewhat sternly. "Why are you so late?"

"How was I supposed to know you had such horrid roads? I nearly broke my leg several times and my dress is covered in dirt!"

Light was beginning to dawn on Jenelle and she asked gently, "What shoes are you wearing, Orlena? Did you wear the ones I had set out beside your chair this morning?"

"Those shoes? Of course not! They may be suitable for dirty work on the ranch, but they do not match this dress and are certainly not acceptable for school!"

"Then which ones did you wear?" Jenelle had seen several pairs of fashionable shoes with high heels and in such colors that no one living on a ranch would think of wearing.

For answer Orlena stuck out her foot to show a very dusty, pale blue shoe with heels two inches high. Norman gave a low whistle when he saw them and shook his head. "No wonder you were late."

Noticing how dirty her shoes were, Orlena turned to her brother, "These will need to be cleaned before tomorrow, Norman. See that one of the hands does a good job, for these are my only blue pair."

"If you want them cleaned, Orlena, you will have to do them yourself. But you won't be wearing them tomorrow."

"And why not?"

"Because you will wear the shoes Jenelle purchased for you so that you can arrive for school on time and make it back home again in time to take care of your chores."

The last words of Norman's brought Orlena to her feet. "Chores?" she exclaimed. "How can you expect me to do chores when I have homework to do?"

"You should have seen the chores I had to do and the stacks of homework." Norman spoke quietly as he turned to hang up his hat. He felt like giving his sister a good scolding for the scare she had given Jenelle, but realizing that it hadn't been intentional, he refrained and only added as he moved towards the stairs, "I'd change those shoes and that dress if I were you before you go take care of the chickens."

"Take care of the chickens?" The indignant surprise in Orlena's voice halted Norman briefly.

"Yes, the chickens. They are your responsibility, remember."

A defiant refusal was on the tip of her tongue, but a sudden remembrance of cleaning the hen house stopped her.

Instead she just slammed her books onto the table and stormed from the house, ignoring the advice about changing her clothes.

Supper that night was somewhat overshadowed by Orlena's sullen manner, and it was a relief when she finished eating and, declaring that she had homework to do, stalked away from the table.

"I wonder how school went today?" Norman murmured as the distant slam of his sister's room sounded.

"I do hope Miss Hearter wasn't too tired out," added Jenelle sympathetically. "Mrs. O'Connor, do you know what her grades were like at her old school?"

Mrs. O'Connor had begun to clear the table but paused to shake her head. "No, I never did see her reports nor hear much about her school achievements. I suspect Norman might know." Then she continued with her task.

Turning to her husband, Jenelle repeated her question for he had apparently been contemplating his glass of water, as he held it in his hand and stared at it.

"Orlena's grades?" he repeated slowly, "I suppose they are with the papers Mr. Athey gave me. Probably in the small trunk. I've been so busy I haven't even looked in there." He set down the glass of water and frowned at it. "Jenelle, I've been too busy."

This plain statement somewhat bewildered Mrs. Mavrich and she could only gaze at him with puzzled eyes. What did being too busy have to do with his sister's grades? And when did Norman ever admit he was too busy? Was he sick? The sudden thought brought instant concern to Jenelle and she spoke gently, "Come into the living room, Dear. It is quite pleasant in the evening and you can rest. Or would you rather go up to bed?"

Pausing in the act of pushing back his chair and standing up, it was Norman's turn to look puzzled. "Bed at this hour? What for? I'm not sick."

"But you said—" began Jenelle.

"That I was too busy," Norman finished with a slight

138

laugh. "I didn't mean I was sick, only too busy." By then the couple had reached the living room. "What I meant was that I haven't taken the time to look into such things as Orlena's grades nor what shoes she has to wear. How could the child have thought she could walk home in those things? Why they are ridiculously out of place!"

A merry laugh followed his outburst and he turned to look at Jenelle.

Her eyes sparkled with merriment and the corners of her mouth twitched.

"I don't know what is so funny," Norman complained as sudden bursts of chuckles still came from his wife though she tried to speak.

"It was the idea of you searching your sister's room to see what kind of shoes she has. And once you discovered some shoes, you wouldn't know if they were street shoes, dance shoes or school shoes nor what kind to get her if you did know." And Jenelle went off into another peal of laughter at the remembrance of Norman's first and only time trying to advise her about what shoes to get. In his ignorance of women's fashions, he had suggested a pair like his own only smaller.

Norman joined in his wife's laughter for he would be among the first to admit that he knew nothing about women's shoes except that the shoes his sister had worn were entirely unfit for much walking.

It wasn't until after their laugh had subsided and all was quiet again that Norman spoke. "I really should go through that trunk and find out her grades. Perhaps tomorrow would work." This last came thoughtfully, and Jenelle knew he was going over the work planned for the following day. "Yes," he continued a moment later, "but it won't be first thing."

Up in her room, Orlena hesitated and stared down at the practical, sturdy shoes Jenelle had bought for her. "Ugly things," she muttered and turned to her closet where she pulled out her rose colored shoes. "I won't wear those things.

They are horrid looking." If her blue shoes from the day before had been unpractical, these rose ones were even more so, thin and low with even narrower heels and large pink bows made of material which spotted should a drop of water fall upon it. How she would be able to leave the house with those shoes on, Orlena wasn't quite certain, but she would not wear the others! Besides, the pink shoes matched her dress.

"Orlena!" a voice called. "Breakfast."

Snatching up her books, Orlena hurried out of her room, for she knew her brother's patience didn't last long if she was late to breakfast.

The patting of her heels on the floor and stairs announced her arrival before she flounced into the room, a rose and cream colored butterfly from the large bows in her hair to the pink ones on her shoes. She looked quite lovely had she been going to a party instead of school.

Norman looked her up and down and his fingers slowly tapped the back of his chair. "Well," he said at last. "Is the governor coming to school this morning?"

For answer, Orlena rolled her eyes in an expression of disgust and prepared to seat herself.

"Just a minute, Orlena." Norman's quiet words stopped her. "I think I mentioned yesterday that you were to wear the shoes Jenelle bought for you."

"I won't need them this morning," was the haughty answer as the princess seated herself. "You or Hardrich can drive me into town and then pick me up after school. Or better yet, hitch up the buggy and I'll drive myself."

Norman's voice was tight as he replied, "You haven't had experience driving these horses and none of the hands, least of all my foreman, can be spared today. You will have to walk. Now go and change your shoes quickly."

Jenelle and Mrs. O'Connor were already seated at the table and each wondered if Orlena would give in without a fight.

Continuing to sit, Orlena tipped her head and asked,

"Why should you care what shoes I wear? You don't have to walk with me."

For a moment Norman turned and looked at the opposite wall, outwardly silent but inwardly praying for wisdom. At last he turned back to his sister; his hands gripped the back of his chair and his fingers were silent. "Orlena, I'll give you a choice. You may either wear the shoes Jenelle bought or I can break the heels off of these and you can wear them."

ℭ

CHAPTER 17

FRESH COURAGE

Orlena's mouth opened but no sound came out. At last she gasped out in a mixture of shock, indignation and unbelief, "Break my shoes? You wouldn't dare!"

"Than go put on the other ones."

"I will not!"

Jenelle watched her husband anxiously, afraid that his temper might get the better of him, but he said nothing. Instead, he walked over and pulled out his sister's chair. Then, still without a word, he stooped, and before Orlena could quite comprehend what he was doing, he had removed the pair of offending shoes from her feet. With one quick move he snapped the heel from one of the dainty, ridiculous pink shoes. Then Orlena found her voice.

"Norman!" she screamed. "You horrid thing! Don't you dare! No!" and she sprang forward to rescue her second shoe from receiving the same fate as the first, but she was too late, for with another snap, the second shoe became almost a slipper.

Giving way to a tantrum as she had only done once before in her brother's presence, she flung herself at him, hitting and kicking while she shrieked every ugly epithet at him that she knew.

Norman had been prepared for an outburst of some sort from this fiery-tempered, thoroughly spoiled, easily infuriated sister, but this was more than he had expected. His surprise at her violent reaction, however, did not slacken his quick response. With strong hands he pinned Orlena's arms to her sides and half carried her back to her chair. There he pushed her down and held her. His jaw was set and his eyes had changed to flashing steel. Not a word was spoken.

Mrs. O'Connor sat in silence, watching and praying. Well she knew that this battle was not just a skirmish, but a major battle, and the one who came off victor would rule in the end. Picking up her fork, Mrs. O'Connor began to eat, outwardly calm, but praying hard all the while that Norman's stock of patience would be able to withstand Orlena's rage.

As for Jenelle, for the first minute, she sat in stunned silence, staring at the drama before her, bewildered. In all her interaction with people, never had she witnessed such a tantrum of temper. How could anyone act like Orlena was acting?

Struggling to free herself from her brother's iron grip, Orlena kept screaming. "I hate you! You are cruel. No one loves me! I want to go back to the city. You can't make me stay here! Let me go!" And then she began calling Norman every name she could think of.

"But we do love you!" Jenelle gasped as once again she heard the cry for love. "We do, oh, if only she would let us show her—" Poor Jenelle, her heart was torn. All she wanted to do was hold her young sister in her arms and cry over her, whisper tender, loving words and do all the things she never got to do to a sister of her own, but she knew as well as Mrs. O'Connor that Norman couldn't give in unless Orlena was going to run the ranch. Finding that she couldn't hold back her tears, Jenelle suddenly rose and fled into the kitchen, out the door and across the yard to the corral. There she leaned against the high fence and sobbed.

A soft nudge against her hair, caused Jenelle to lift her head. "Hello, Girl," she whispered, reaching up to stroke the face of the nut-brown horse who had come over to see what the commotion was about. "It's all a mess, and I don't know what to do."

The horse gave a soft whicker as of sympathy and nuzzled her shoulder.

Giving a watery smile, Jenelle leaned her face against the horse's neck struggling with her tears.

"Mrs. Mavrich?"

"Yes, Lloyd?" Jenelle didn't turn her head.

"Is . . . is everything all right? I saw you come out and—" here the hired hand hesitated, not sure how to say what he meant. "I mean if there's anything I can do . . ." His voice trailed off.

"There is something."

"Anything, Ma'am."

She didn't look at him but answered in a voice that was full of tears, "Pray, Lloyd, pray."

"Yes, Ma'am, I will." The soft tramp of his boots sounded as he turned and moved away towards the bunkhouse where the other men were finishing their breakfast and preparing for the day's work.

Jim Hardrich beckoned the young hand. "How's Mrs. Mavrich?"

Lloyd shrugged. "She didn't say, but she's been crying. She just told me to pray. I don't like it, Mr. Hardrich. There's got to be something wrong if Mr. Mavrich isn't out with her."

"You didn't see him anywhere?"

Lloyd shook his head.

For a moment the foreman stood silent and thoughtful, his face serious. At last he spoke. "I'll be back," was all he said before striding away towards the corral.

Jenelle was softly stroking the horse's face and neck as he approached. "Mrs. Mavrich," the deep voice was quiet. "Is Norman almost through with breakfast?"

Turning from the horse at the words of the older foreman, Jenelle's chin quivered. "I don't know! He hadn't even gotten to take a bite of it when I came out. Oh, what are we going to do?"

Mr. Hardrich didn't pretend not to know what the

small woman before him was talking about. He knew. "We're going to keep on praying."

"Are you praying for Norman too?"

Reaching out, he placed one of his large rough hands on Jenelle's arm. "Mrs. Mavrich, we're praying for each of you, and we're going to keep right on praying until the answer comes."

Drawing a deep breath, Jenelle whispered, "Thank you."

All was quiet for a moment save for the sounds of the birds and the restless movement of some of the horses in the other corral. Breaking the silence Mr. Hardrich spoke calmly, "Just tell Mr. Mavrich that I've taken the men out past Crystal Creek and he needn't come out unless he wishes to. One hand more or less won't make a difference." Jenelle nodded and the ranch foreman added, "And remember the Lord is faithful."

"I will. Thank you, Mr. Hardrich. You have helped me. I won't forget." She pressed the rough hand in both her own and the smile she gave was peaceful.

After watching the foreman stride away, Jenelle gave one final pat to the horse and turned towards the house. All was quiet when she reached the kitchen and, picking up a basket, she hummed as she walked over to the chicken coop. Gathering the eggs each morning was a task she had always enjoyed and after turning the care of the chickens over to Orlena, she had often missed it. Now her humming became a song.

> "God moves in a mysterious way
> His wonders to perform;
> He plants His footsteps in the sea
> And rides upon the storm.
>
> Ye fearful saints, fresh courage take;
> The clouds ye so much dread
> Are big with mercy, and shall break

In blessings on your head."

She was latching the gate of the chicken pen when someone took her basket of eggs. Looking around she saw Norman. Instantly her song ended and she looked anxiously into his tired face. "What happened?" Jenelle was almost afraid to ask.

"She's on her way to school. But you shouldn't be doing her chores. Are you all right?"

"Of course, and I wanted to gather the eggs. I've missed it."

Together in silence they walked back to the house, Norman carrying the basket of eggs. Setting down the basket on the table, Norman followed his wife back out into the morning sunshine. The quiet calm of the morning soothed his taut spirit, and feeling the sympathetic silence of Jenelle beside him, he let out a deep sigh. "What are we going to do? If I had thought there'd be this much trouble, I might have—Well, I don't know what I would have done." Norman's voice spoke of the conflict he had just been through and with another sigh, he leaned against a large tree.

"We knew it would be difficult when we agreed to bring her here."

"Yes," he agreed, "but not this difficult."

Jenelle softly hummed the hymn which had been running through her head as she leaned lovingly against her husband's arm. "The bud may have a bitter taste, but sweet will be the flower," she quoted musingly. "It will all come right, Norman. Mr. Hardrich reminded me this morning that God is faithful. Let us keep on praying and working, and in due season we shall reap, if we faint not."

Norman didn't reply right away. He was remembering something his uncle used to tell him. "Norm, you can't expect to train a wild horse in a day. You have to do it over time, but if you are faithful, calm, and earn their trust, you'll win out every time."

"Oh, Norman," Jenelle's quiet voice brought him back

from the past. "Mr. Hardrich said to tell you he took the men past Crystal Creek and for you not to bother to go out unless you want to."

Norman started. "Crystal Creek? Jenelle, I completely forgot about the work planned for today! I ought to saddle up and ride out there right away." He turned to head to the barn but his wife held him back.

"Why must you go? Mr. Hardrich said he didn't need you."

"But I should be out there working, Dear. After all, this is our ranch."

"Then I should go too."

"Why?"

Jenelle looked up. "Because I'm part of the ranch and if you can't even spare a day . . ."

At that Norman smiled. "All right, I get the point. I suppose it won't hurt the ranch if I spend a day around the house. If I stay here I should look through those papers from Grandmother's lawyer."

Arm in arm the master and mistress of Triple Creek Ranch slowly strolled back to the house from which they had come with such troubled hearts and minds. Those thoughts weren't entirely banished though no expression on either face betrayed the fact. Lurking not far from the surface in the mind of each, the perplexing problems of Orlena ran and tumbled endlessly like a turbulent little stream seeking a peaceful lake into which to settle and be at rest. Would that peacefulness ever come? What else must they endure before it was reached?

It was a quiet morning for the most part. Norman and Jenelle went through the papers in the trunk and discovered Orlena's grades were rather average. When Norman suggested looking at Orlena's shoes, Jenelle shook her head. "No, Dear, I don't think that would be wise. She would notice and feel that we don't trust her."

"Do we?" Norman's eyebrows raised in surprise.

"We try to." Sitting down on the bed and tucking one

foot under her, Jenelle looked earnestly at her husband. "I do feel sorry for Orlena."

"Sorry for her! Still? Jenelle, really—"

"But I do," interrupted Jenelle. "I've been thinking about her a lot this morning and trying to put myself in her place. Norman, those fancy dresses and shoes aren't for our benefit, they are to impress her classmates in hopes of making them her friends. She won't admit it, probably not even to herself, but she's afraid."

Leaning back against the doorframe with his thumbs tucked in his belt, Norman looked down at his small wife in disbelief. "Afraid? Orlena? Really, Jenelle, she's a spoiled brat who thinks the whole world revolves around her whims and hasn't a care unless things don't go her way."

The quiet, positive shake of Mrs. Mavrich's head and her softly repeated words, "She's afraid," caused Norman to ask, "Of what?"

"Everything. She's afraid her classmates won't accept her, afraid she might have to display her ignorance before everyone, afraid of all the changes life has been bringing her, afraid that she won't ever be loved."

With a single step, Norman was beside Jenelle. Lifting her face up he stooped and kissed her, saying softly, "Your empathy is beyond my comprehension, but I love you for it! Let's pray for our sister right now." Together they knelt in prayer. And Mrs. O'Connor, coming upstairs and hearing those prayers, slipped into her own room and also knelt, while far out in the fields past Crystal Creek, Hardrich, Hearter, St. John, Alden and the other hands went about their work with prayers in their hearts.

After lunch, Norman headed out to the corral to work with one of the young horses. Jenelle, always a lover of horses, went along to watch. There the problems of Orlena were pushed away and all their thoughts were about the horse, a beautiful young filly Jenelle had named Minuet for the dainty, prancing way she moved.

"I'll tell you one thing, Jenelle," Norman spoke with conviction as he kept the horse trotting around the corral, "this horse is going to be a good cutter once she gets trained."

As though in agreement, Minuet tossed her head and snorted. Jenelle, leaning against the fence, laughed. "Then I want her, Norman."

"You?"

"I don't have a cutter, but I used to help with the round-ups back home. And look, she even knows my voice." It was true; at the sound of Jenelle's voice, Minuet had pricked up her ears and, though she kept going around the corral, her ears swiveled to catch every word Jenelle said.

"Perhaps I should leave her to you to train for riding," Norman grinned, slowing the horse to a walk. "I don't have much time for working with her anyway."

Before Jenelle could reply, Minuet halted suddenly, tossed her head and gave a whinny, her dainty forefeet pawing the ground.

"Whoa there, girl. Easy now," Norman soothed. "Steady." He grasped the halter as he talked quietly to the nervous horse. "Jenelle, she hears something. Can you tell what it is?"

Jenelle turned in the direction Minuet's ears were pointed. "A wagon is turning into the lane. Looks like Mr. Bittner, Norman and . . . I think he has Orlena with him!"

Quickly Norman took the lead rope off Minuet's bridle and left the corral to meet the approaching wagon.

"Howdy, Mavrich, Misses," their neighbor greeted them, touching his hat to Mrs. Mavrich as he spoke. "Was headin' out of town and saw your sister leavin' school. Thought I'd save her a walk home since I was plannin' on stoppin' here anyhow."

Orlena, having gathered her books and lunch pail, accepted her brother's help from the high wagon seat and, turning to Mr. Bittner said pertly, "Thank you for the ride."

"Any time, Miss," and Mr. Bittner touched his hat once

again as Orlena flounced into the house, her dark curls bouncing on her shoulders.

"You wanted to see me, Bittner?" Norman pushed back his hat and waited.

"Yep, I got a round-up set for next week and I don't have enough hands. Can you spare any of yours for a few days?"

"Sure I can. I promised Carmond some help the following week and Peterson over at Broken K as well. But I can spare some next week. How many will you need?"

Bittner shook his head. "I can't rightly say, but I'll take all the help I can get since I added more cattle in the spring. By the way, when are you plannin' your round-up, Mavrich?"

"I don't know for sure. Not for another two or three weeks. We have some fences we need to fix before we move them. By the way, have you talked to Bates about his round-up? Back in the spring I told him to let me know when he was going to start this fall and I'd bring some help over. I've been busy with work around here and haven't seen him in town when I've been there."

"I'll stop by and check," Bittner offered. "He's not much out of my way. Nice place he has too, that Rising B, though not the spread you've got here." Mr. Bittner cast admiring eyes about the well kept grounds of the Triple Creek.

"I can't take the credit," Norman smiled. "Uncle Hiram did a fine job building this place up."

"That he did. A fine job. But I'd best be gettin' on now. I'll let you know what I find out from Bates. Good day, Mavrich, Mrs. Mavrich." Mr. Bittner touched his hat to Jenelle once again as he started his horses for home.

CHAPTER 18

ROUND-UP PLANS

As the dust settled behind the big rancher, Norman scratched his ear and remarked, "It looks like the busy days are again before us, Darling."

"But not as busy as in spring."

"True." A nicker from the corral behind them made Norman say, "But I'm not going to get anything done if I stand around and talk with you. Minuet needs some more work before I call it a day." He kissed her quickly and Jenelle watched him stride back to the corral.

Supper that evening was a quiet affair. Orlena spoke nothing except for monosyllables when a direct question was put to her by Jenelle. Her brother she ignored completely. She had decided on the way to school that if he was only going to treat her like a servant, she would just ignore him. She wished she dared neglect the chores he had assigned her, but here she hesitated. Would it be worth the struggle? At length she decided that it wouldn't and hoped that her silence would be enough to cause Norman to yield to her wishes. The air of aloof superiority she had assumed ever since Norman had come inside continued throughout the evening.

"'Tis a fine state of things to be sure, Norman," Mrs. O'Connor sniffed after Orlena had gone to her room, ignoring her brother's existence completely.

"It won't be the first time Orlena has pretended I don't

exist. You surely remember that, Mrs. O'Connor. And if I know my sister, it won't be the last."

"I still say 'tis a state of things entirely!"

"But you must admit it's more peaceful when she doesn't talk," and Norman smiled slightly. His sister's silent treatment of him had not bothered him, he merely wondered how long it would last.

T

Several days passed and Orlena kept up her silence. This was a difficult thing to do, for her love of talking or complaining was strong; however, she was determined not to yield until her brother agreed to follow her wishes. She never stopped to consider that he might not comply with her desires, for always before when she had treated her grandmother to silence, she always gave in before long or pacified her granddaughter in another way.

As for her shoes, Orlena, having reached the conclusion that her city shoes would no longer work for walking to school, decided to wear the ones Jenelle had purchased for her. This decision was perhaps partially reached because every other girl at school, including the teacher, wore the same kind of shoes which Jenelle had purchased for her. Even after she had decided, it was hard to put them on. Her face was fierce when she came down to breakfast the first morning with them on and had someone commented on them, she no doubt would have rushed right back to her room to replace them. As it was, however, no one said a word or seemed to so much as glance at her attire. She wondered why, when Norman had made it such a point only the day before. Never would she have dreamed that the very sound of her heels on the stairs told Norman and Jenelle what shoes she had chosen to wear.

T

On Saturday Mr. Bittner stopped by. It was evening and Norman had just arrived back at the house.

"I stopped at the Risin' B," Triple Creek's visitor said, "and Bates was want'n to get his cattle rounded up and start cuttin' on Monday. His ranch isn't that big an' I reckon I can spare some of my hands to help him and then start my own in the middle of the week. What do you say, Mavrich? Can you spare that many hands for the week?"

For a moment Norman scratched his chin and then looked over at his foreman. "Jim, do you think we can finish getting ready without all the hands? We already promised help for the following week at Running C and Broken K. That'll give us two weeks before we're ready to even start."

Hardrich nodded. "I reckon if you leave St. John and Scott, the four of us can finish if we put in some long days."

"What about Hearter? I thought you'd want him?" Norman knew Hardrich had taken to the young hand in a special way since Lloyd's father had died a few years back.

"He's good with horses. Besides, he's got a fine cutter and likes the saddle and ropes better than he does the fences and posts."

The men laughed and Norman turned to Mr. Bittner. "Well, so be it. I'll send the men over to the Rising B on Monday and once they're finished over there they can head over to your place."

Mr. Bittner held out his hand. "I say that's mighty generous of you, Mavrich. You just let the word out when you're ready to round up your own and we'll all be over to lend a hand."

Shaking hands, Norman chuckled. "We might end up with more cowboys than cattle. The Triple Creek isn't that large."

And so the busy days of the fall round-ups began, not only for Triple Creek Ranch but for all the surrounding ranches. Often the work began before sunrise and ended only after the sun had set in the west. So busy were the few men left on Triple Creek, that Norman was scarcely seen by the women in the house and Orlena's silent treatment went on with Norman scarcely noticing. Jenelle took over all the milking each day, though Norman protested.

"Quit fussing," Jenelle scolded him with a smile. "I can milk three cows twice a day for a few weeks. Goodness, Norman, one would think I had grown up in the city with a house full of servants the way you are acting! Get on with your own work and let me do the things I can."

Mrs. O'Connor took over the entire care of the house, leaving Jenelle free not just to milk the cows but also to work with Minuet while the menfolk were gone. Often Mrs. O'Connor would look out the door to see Jenelle, her light hair twisted up into a bun, standing in the middle of the corral while the young horse trotted around her. Coming in later, Jenelle would sink down onto a chair, pushing back the loose pieces of windblown hair from her flushed face while her eyes sparkled with life. To her housekeeper's caution not to "work too hard," Mrs. Mavrich only laughed. She was thoroughly enjoying her activities.

T

Over two weeks had passed since Mr. Bittner had first talked to Norman Mavrich about the fall round-ups. Many of the ranches in the area of Rough Rock had already finished their cattle selling and, with their now smaller herds, were beginning to prepare for winter. It was a lovely Sunday afternoon and the tang in the air brought with it a feeling of energy, of an eagerness to be out and doing.

"Mavrich!"

Norman turned his head as he, Jenelle, Orlena and Mrs. O'Connor stepped from the church. A shorter man, stocky and with the walk of a cowboy, crossed the street towards them.

"Good morning, Bates," Norman greeted the man with a smile.

"Just wanted to thank you for lendin' me those hands of yours. They sure know how to get a job done. And that young fellow, Hearter, he and his pony can cut cattle faster than anyone I've ever seen."

"I can't argue with that," Norman agreed. "He's good all right."

"Well," the rancher of the Rising B continued, "I hear most everyone else is done with their round-up. When you plannin' on startin?"

"I'm thinking it will be Tuesday. We still have a few things to get finished before we start and I figure we can get them taken care of tomorrow."

"Why don't some of us ranchers here get a few hands and come over this afternoon and give you a hand? What do you say, men?" And Mr. Bates turned to look questioningly at the few other ranchers who, hearing the sound of ranch talk, had joined the two men.

As several ranchers began nodding, Norman smiled and shook his head. "I'll say that's mighty kind of all of you, but I can't use anyone today."

"Why not?" Mr. Bates was puzzled.

"Today is the Lord's day, Bates," Norman said quietly. "Those of us on Triple Creek Ranch don't do unnecessary work on Sunday."

"But Mavrich," protested Bates, "your round-up's mighty important and so gettin' the other work done becomes a necessary thing."

"It can wait until tomorrow. Today is set aside to honor the Lord and rest from our labors. And," Norman flashed a smile from his sun tanned face, "we can use a day of rest! But come Tuesday, I'll take any help I can get. It's going to be quite a job finding and bringing in all the cattle with the size of my place and the terrain I've got."

"We'll be there," Mr. Carmond assured him.

"Count on some from the Silver Spur."

"And the Broken K."

Mr. Bates still looked puzzled. "Well, Mavrich, I don't yet understand, but my sons an' I'll be at the Triple Creek on Tuesday."

When Norman reached the wagon, he found the ladies already seated and waiting for him. Quickly he took his seat and picked up the reins.

It wasn't until they had left the small town of Rough Rock that anyone spoke.

"What did Mr. Bates want?" Jenelle asked.

"He was offering to get some other men and come over this afternoon to help get the last things done so we could start the round-up in the morning."

"What did you tell him?"

"I thanked him but said Triple Creek didn't do extra work on Sundays. We'll finish the work tomorrow and start the round-up on Tuesday."

Jenelle nodded, satisfied.

From the seat behind came Orlena's voice, "Norman Mavrich, you certainly have some queer notions. Why on earth won't you let some others come over and work on Sunday if they want to? Sunday is just another day except it is considered "the thing" to go to church.

At the start of Orlena's outburst, Norman glanced over at Jenelle, a slight grin twitching the corners of his mouth. It was the first time Orlena had spoken directly to him since the shoe trouble. Only the other day he had told his wife, "Don't worry about it, she'll break the silence herself one of these days." He had been right. However, he wisely refrained from alluding to that fact as he answered Orlena.

"Sunday is the Lord's day, Orlena. It is also God's appointed day of rest. In the ten commandments it says, 'Remember the Sabbath day to keep it holy. Six days shalt thou labor and do all thy work but the seventh is the Sabbath of the Lord thy God.' You see, Orlena, the Lord created a day that was to be set aside for Him. A day when work was to be laid aside and men were to praise and worship their Creator."

Orlena snorted and muttered, "If you want to waste another day just because of some foolish notion from ages ago, it's not my problem."

At the breakfast table on Monday, Norman ate quickly. He knew it would be a busy day if he wanted things ready to start the round-up the following morning. Even though he was rushed, he still took time to give some directions and information before heading off to work. "The rest of the hands should be getting back today," he began, "so I'm expecting everyone here for supper. And there might be some extras. Carmond mentioned on Saturday that he and his men might be coming this evening so as to be here for the early start in the morning." He paused and thought. "You know, it might be best if we all ate in the bunk house dining room tonight. There'd be more room and if any of the other ranches send men this evening, I'd like to have enough places for them. Mrs. O'Connor, I'm going to be sending St. John back this afternoon to help prepare the supper. Sorry I can't spare more men, but—"

Mrs. O'Connor interrupted. "Now don't be fretting about that. St. John is the right help I'll be needing entirely."

"And I'll be able to help them as well, Dear," Jenelle put in brightly.

"Good. Orlena," he turned to his sister, "I'm expecting you at supper tonight as well. There will be a lot going on in the next days or weeks and I want everyone there tonight."

"I don't eat with hired hands." Orlena looked haughtily at her brother. "And I won't eat in a bunk house."

Norman returned her look steadily as he replied, "You will eat with whoever is there tonight and you will eat in the bunk house." Turning to Jenelle he held out his coffee cup. "One more cup, Jenelle, then I must get a move on."

CHAPTER 19

THE LONELIEST TIMES

Orlena hadn't meant to obey her brother and eat with the hired hands in the bunk house, but remembering the look in his eyes and feeling as though she would get the worst of a struggle at this time, she made her reluctant appearance. To her intense disgust, Lloyd was seated across the table from her. The remembrance of their first meeting still rankled in her mind and she wished again that she could get even with him.

There were many extra men at the table that night. Not only had men from the Running C come, but several other ranches had sent men who could be spared from morning chores to get ready for the big day.

It would take several days to ride out and begin the cattle drive towards the corrals. There would be long, hard days in the saddle before they even came to the cutting and sorting of the cattle. Then would come the drive to the stockyards near the station where the cattle to be sold would be loaded on the trains. There were several other large ranches in the area, but none quite as large or as well stocked with cattle as the Triple Creek Ranch. When Norman's Uncle Hiram had started it over fifty years before, it was the first ranch around those parts. Since then Triple Creek's brand had become well known for its fine beef and honest dealings, and it was an honor for cowhands to say they had worked for or on the Triple Creek Ranch.

Evening came and as darkness settled over the ranch, the lights in the bunk house went out as the men turned in for a good sleep in preparation for many days of hard work and beds on the ground.

In the ranch house, the only light still burning was in the room of Mr. and Mrs. Mavrich.

Jenelle was leaning against her husband, her face hidden on his shirt. They had just risen from their knees and Norman had wrapped his arms about his little wife.

"I know I'll be gone for several days, Jenelle, but I'll be careful, you know I will. Now," he added, softly looking down at the top of her light head, "you won't worry about me, will you?"

A muffled voice answered, "Of course I will." Then, looking up, she smiled tenderly as she whispered, "But I'll miss you even more."

"I love you, Sweetheart!" Their lips met in a long kiss before Norman reached for the light. "Let's get to bed. I've got to be up mighty early tomorrow."

The noise of horses whinnying, saddles jingling, the shouts of men and a general sound of confusion roused Orlena much earlier then she ever remembered awakening. Her room was slightly chilly and, scrambling out of bed, she pulled a warm morning wrapper about her before hurrying to the window. It was still rather dark, but to the east a faint line of pink showed where the sun would soon be coming forth from its nightly tour of the European and Asian countries. Below, near the barns, several lanterns were lit, and Orlena could see horses being saddled, and men already mounted and gathered in groups.

"Surely that can't be Jenelle out there?" she gasped in surprise as she saw the slight form of her sister-in-law moving from group to group. "What is she doing out so early?" Orlena shook her head. "These people must be mad!" Never had she seen anything like it and, in spite of her criticism, she

continued to watch in fascination, for there was something that held her nearly spellbound at the sight of so many cowboys and horses. At last she saw Norman kiss Jenelle before swinging up into his saddle.

"Let's go!" His words rang out on the morning air and the crowd of men rode off into the early morning with a trampling of hooves, a jingle of bridles and the shouts of some of the cowboys. The fall cattle round-up of Triple Creek Ranch had begun and from the looks of the morning sky, it would be beautiful weather.

Orlena watched until the riders were lost over the hills and then turned away with a little sigh. The departure had looked so grand and exciting, but now everything was quiet again.

Later, the three womenfolk ate their breakfast in almost complete silence. Jenelle's mind was with her husband, wondering what was happening and, most of all, when the men would return.

Busy with plans for the day, Mrs. O'Connor wasn't worried about the round-up. She knew so little about one that the thought of danger never crossed her mind. There was enough to do at the house, and besides, since the men were all going to be gone for at least a few days, Mrs. O'Connor was planning on washing all the bedding in the bunk house and giving it a good cleaning.

"Jenelle," Mrs. O'Connor broke into Jenelle's thoughts. "When was the last time the bunk house got a good scrubbing?"

"The bunk house? I don't know. I know I've never done it. I've been too busy. But it can't be too bad for Norman and Mr. Hardrich see to it that the men clean it once a month."

Mrs. O'Connor snorted softly. "Once a month. 'Tis not likely to be clean as it should be. Quite a job it will be entirely, but Margaret Patrick O'Connor is not one to be leaving things dirty."

There was no answer to this, for Jenelle's mind was with the riders again and as for Orlena, her thoughts were still on the sight of all those men riding off into the morning light.

T

Several long days passed to those waiting at the ranch house. Each one seemed longer than the last to Mrs. Mavrich who missed her husband greatly. Mrs. O'Connor pressed her into service in a thorough cleaning of the bunk house, which helped somewhat, as it occupied many hours of her days and left her tired. Other times she spent working with Minuet, but still the days dragged. Often Mrs. O'Connor would find her standing and gazing out over the empty pasture.

"This is the only thing about ranch life that I'm not fond of, Mrs. O'Connor; this waiting at the house for days while the men are out doing the round-up. Several times when I was younger, my father would let me help with part of the round-up on our ranch. He never would let me go very far, but I got a taste of what it is like. Now I have to wait and wonder where they are and what they are doing . . ." her voice trailed off and she turned towards the house.

At last, one afternoon, Mrs. O'Connor was startled by an excited Jenelle who came rushing into the kitchen.

"They're coming, Mrs. O'Connor! The first group will be here soon. I just saw some dust off near North Creek."

"The men are back? All of them?"

"Oh no, only a few, but they'll be hungry and tired after such long days in the saddle."

Mrs. O'Connor looked at Jenelle's excited, flushed face. "I don't know if I can have anything ready in a few minutes—" she began.

"We have at least an hour before they'll get here. It takes a while to drive cattle especially ones that are going to be sold. If you move them too quickly they'll lose weight,"

Jenelle explained, her eyes bright with anticipation; the waiting was almost over.

"In that case, let's get busy," and Mrs. O'Connor handed an apron to Jenelle.

As Jenelle had predicted, it was over an hour before three horsemen clattered into the yard and dismounted. Quickly Jenelle hurried out to greet them, wondering and half hoping that one of the men would be her husband but feeling sure none of them would be. Norman would have gone to the farthest corner of the farthest pasture himself, for he never would ask his men to do what he wouldn't do himself. That was one of the reasons his men respected him so much.

Orlena, having come home from school in time to hear of the coming riders, looked out her bedroom window. Somehow those three tired and dirty looking cowboys didn't have the same appeal to her as they had when they rode away. "This place is just horrid," she muttered with a frown. "All this excitement about gathering a bunch of dirty cows together. Why don't they just bring the ones they want to sell? Or better yet? Why doesn't Norman just sell the whole place and move to the city? The honorable Norman Mavrich, an exceptional lawyer. I could be proud of him then. But now— Humph!" and she turned away in disgust.

"Howdy, Mrs. Mavrich," Alden greeted Jenelle as she came over to the returned men.

"Welcome back," she smiled. "How did it go?"

"We didn't have any trouble. Brought back twenty-seven head," replied Alden as he and his companions swung down off their mounts and began to unsaddle them.

The two other men were from neighboring ranches, and Jenelle didn't know them very well. "I suppose you three are ready for clean clothes and a hot meal. Just unsaddle the horses and I'll take care of them while you head to the bunk house to get cleaned up. Mrs. O'Connor will have supper for you in the kitchen as soon as you are ready for it."

"Mrs. Mavrich," Alden protested, "we can feed our mounts. There's no need for you to do it."

Placing her hands on her hips, Jenelle tried to look stern, but the corners of her mouth kept turning up. "I gave you three an order." Then she coaxed, "Oh, let me, please. I know there's no need for me to feed the horses, but I want to. I can't just stand around and watch. I promise it won't be too hard. I've been taking care of the other horses."

It was hard not to give in but still Alden hesitated. "But Mr. Mavrich won't—"

"He'd understand and hurry off for clean clothes and Mrs. O'Connor's cooking if I offered," Jenelle countered, knowing the men wouldn't refuse her.

One of the horses bobbed his head as though in agreement and Jenelle laughed. "There, you see, Todd? Even Strawberry Girl understands and agrees. Now get along with you."

"Yes, Ma'am!" Alden knew better than to argue with the boss's wife. "Come on fellas, I can smell Mrs. O'Connor's supper now!"

After rubbing down and feeding the horses, Jenelle paused a moment to stroke Minuet's nose as the horse leaned over the corral fence and nickered. "The others will be coming along now in small groups of two and three," she whispered. "And in one of them will come Norman." She gave a sigh and turned to look towards the far fields. "The loneliest times of a rancher's wife are during the spring and fall round-ups." Gently the horse blew into Jenelle's face. "I know, at least this time I have Mrs. O'Connor and Orlena. Speaking of Orlena," Jenelle turned and looked up at her sister's window where a light gleamed. "I wonder if she'll be down for supper tonight since some of the men are back."

Orlena did come down but ate alone in the dining room while the others sat and talked in the kitchen. Jenelle, having grown up on a ranch, wanted to hear all about the men's experience and Mrs. O'Connor listened in wonder.

"When do you think the others will be back?" Jenelle

asked at last as Alden and the other men were preparing to head off to the bunk house for the night.

Alden shrugged. "There's no tellin' ma'am. I'm thinkin' some of the others will be along tomorrow, but it's a long way to the far end of the ranch and it'll take even longer to drive the cattle in."

"I know," Jenelle sighed. After a moment of silence, she drew a deep breath and smiled. "If more are coming in tomorrow, we'd all best be heading to bed soon. Are you going to start cutting the cattle tomorrow?"

Alden shook his head. "Not unless Hardrich or Mr. Mavrich come in. If it were just branding, we'd get started, but— They know what's being sold this year."

ℂ

CHAPTER 20

"I'LL BE VERY CAREFUL"

The following afternoon found two other groups of riders coming in with cattle. One of the riders was Lloyd. Being the youngest hand on Triple Creek sometimes had its disadvantages, but not when it came to Mrs. Mavrich. She was a firm friend and he seemed to feel as though she were one of his older sisters. Often he had volunteered to help her out around the house, and he was the one she would send into town on errands for her with permission to stop by and visit his mother. Mrs. Hearter wasn't very well and Jenelle knew Lloyd's visits cheered her up.

"Howdy, Mrs. Mavrich!"

Jenelle turned from the corral where she had been talking to Minuet. "Well, Lloyd, welcome back. How was the round-up?"

"Just fine exceptin' we weren't doin' any cutting an' Spitfire complained about it."

Shaking her head with a smile at the young hand's words, Jenelle replied, "Well, it won't be too long before the two of you can do all the cutting of cattle you'd like."

A nicker of agreement from Minuet interrupted and Lloyd stepped over to the fence. Talking softly, he reached out his hand and stroked her neck. "She's certainly going to be a fine horse to train."

"Mr. Mavrich says she'll be a good cutter," began

169

Jenelle, but Minuet again interrupted the conversation. Unexpectedly she flung up her head and side stepped quickly. Then, with head tossing and feet prancing nervously, she backed away from the fence, snorting.

Mrs. Mavrich and Lloyd turned quickly to see Orlena approaching. There was a look of disgust on her face.

"I might have known you'd be out here with that stupid animal," she remarked with disdain. The presence of Lloyd didn't sweeten her temper any.

"Were you looking for me, Orlena?" Jenelle asked quietly.

"*I* wasn't, it's Mrs. O'Connor. Though why she thought *I* could be interrupted from my work any easier than she could, just shows that she isn't well educated."

"When did you arrive home from school?"

"I just arrived and haven't the time to come all the way out here looking for you. One would think that you had enough education to know where you belonged."

Jenelle could tell by a quick glance at the young man beside her that he was having a hard time keeping still. It would never do if he lost his temper so she spoke quickly. "Tell Mrs. O'Connor I'll be right in. And thank you, Orlena, for coming to find me."

With a haughty toss of her head, Orlena flounced back to the house.

After she was gone, Jenelle turned to Lloyd who stood watching Minuet while he gripped the fence fiercely. "Forget all that went on just now," Jenelle spoke softly.

"But Mrs. Mavrich! That child shouldn't . . . How dare she . . ."

"I know Lloyd, but listen to me." She placed a hand on his arm and her voice was firm. "Orlena is just like the rest of us. We are all sinners and before Christ saved us, we too were capable of acting just like she did. Orlena doesn't know Jesus Christ. She's never had much experience with any who do know Him either, so she's watching us, Lloyd, to see how we respond. She doesn't know that what she is missing in her life is the Heavenly Father, so don't let your anger over a small thing that doesn't matter get the better of you and cause your witness for Him to be spoiled. When you feel this way, pray for her, Lloyd. Pray hard."

The earnest appeal of Jenelle's words spoke to the young man's heart and his anger died away. "I'll do that, Ma'am," he replied softly. "I'll pray for her and try to keep my temper from gettin' the best of me."

"Thank you, Lloyd. Now, I know you've been riding for days, but if you'd like, you can ride into town to see your mother. I know she'd like that."

"I'd like that too, Mrs. Mavrich, but . . ." he turned to look at the young horse still prancing about the corral.

Jenelle knew at once what he was thinking and, knowing her husband would have no objections since it was Lloyd, spoke again. "Spitfire might need a rest before you get to work again, but Minuet is in need of exercise. Norman's ridden her a few times, but has never had much time for more. Though I've been working with her, I haven't ridden her. Suppose you ride Minuet into town and see how she does."

"You really mean that, Mrs. Mavrich, Ma'am?"

Mrs. Mavrich nodded. "And Lloyd," she called after the rapidly retreating form. Lloyd stopped and turned. "If you would like, stay and have supper with your mother and sisters. Just don't be too late getting back."

"Yes, Ma'am. No, Ma'am. Thank you, Mrs. Mavrich!" And Lloyd disappeared into the barn for his saddle.

Laughing, Jenelle hurried to the house. "I don't know which the lad is most eager about, getting to see his mother or riding Minuet."

The sun was setting and it was growing dark before Lloyd returned to Triple Creek Ranch. Throwing a light shawl about her shoulders, Mrs. Mavrich hurried out to join the group of men about the rider and horse. She was as anxious as they were to see how Minuet had behaved. Lloyd had dismounted and was unsaddling her as Jenelle approached.

"She still needs work, but she's a fine horse." Just then Lloyd caught sight of Jenelle. "Mr. Mavrich was right, Ma'am," he exclaimed, patting Minuet's neck. "She's going to be a fine cutter once she gets some training. I'd say almost as fine as Spitfire." Coming from Lloyd that was high praise, for all the hands knew he considered his horse the best in those parts.

T

The sound of cattle lowing, of calves bawling, the thudding of horses hooves and now and then a sharp whinny, cattlemen shouting and calling all blended together to make a confused noise that never seemed to end. Jenelle didn't mind it; in fact, she delighted in those sounds, for they all spoke of a successful round-up. True to her predictions, Norman had been the last to arrive back at the ranch, but now he was home and the job of cutting, sorting and preparing the cattle for sale or for the coming winter had begun. All the owners from the neighboring ranches had returned to their own spreads, leaving as many hands as the Triple Creek could use until the job was completed and the cattle which were to be shipped out by train, had been driven to the stockyards outside of town.

It was during one of the busy afternoons, when Mrs. O'Connor, St. John and Jenelle were all three busy in the ranch kitchen, that Jenelle saw a horse and rider approaching the back of the house. Wiping her hands on her apron she stepped out to see who the visitor could be, for she knew no one with the cattle would notice a newcomer.

"Good afternoon, Mrs. Mavrich," a bright cheery voice called as a young girl slipped from the horse.

"Why Katie, this is a pleasant surprise. What brings you out to Triple Creek Ranch? I thought you were away at school?"

The girl laughed pleasantly. "Oh I was, but you see, we have a holiday for two weeks because Mrs. Simpson, the head mistress, was thrown from her carriage last week and has suffered a broken leg, and Miss Lindsey had to return home to help her family through a crisis of some sort and so, here I am!"

"I do hope Mrs. Simpson will soon be well again," Jenelle sympathized.

"Oh, yes, the doctor says so, but he thought it best for her to have complete rest for two weeks. And since Uncle David and Aunt Winnie were already gone on a business trip to the east, I was allowed to come home." Katie's eyes moved across the yard to where the forms of cattle, horses and men moved continually. "I suppose it wouldn't be possible for me to see Lloyd for a few minutes, would it, Mrs. Mavrich? I know this isn't a good time, but—"

Jenelle couldn't help smiling at the anxious face of her young visitor. "Of course it would. I know Mr. Mavrich wouldn't mind if Lloyd took a break to visit with his favorite sister for a little while. Especially since he hasn't seen her for many months."

"Oh, I'm not his favorite sister," Katie began. "That would be Connie."

"I'm not so sure about that, Katie. All he talks about when he returns from a visit into town is what you've written in your last letter."

Katie blushed and smiled. "Even if I'm not his favorite sister, he's my favorite brother! Where is he, Mrs. Mavrich?"

Before Jenelle could answer, Orlena swept out of the house. She had seen the visitor from inside and wondering who she was, had come out to see. She could tell that the visitor was from the city and not a neighboring ranch for her hat and clothes, though rather plain, had the look of the city about them.

Jenelle turned to her with a smile, "Orlena, I'd like you to meet Katie Hearter. Katie, this is my sister, Orlena Mavrich."

"How do you do, Orlena." Katie smiled and held out her hand. "You must just love living on such a large spread as this!"

Orlena took the offered hand and murmured something indistinct as Katie continued.

"Lloyd says that he's going to have a ranch as big as this someday. Of course he may be fifty before he gets one this large," she laughed gaily. "Mrs. Mavrich, he told me once that I could take care of his house for him until he finds a wife. I wonder how long that will be because he'll never find himself a wife out in the middle of the cattle pasture or the range." And again her bright laugh rang out.

Jenelle laughed also, it was nearly impossible not to with someone as bright and merry as Katie Hearter. "Orlena," Jenelle turned to her sister who was standing silently beside her, "could you please take Katie out and help her locate Lloyd? I would but I must get back to the kitchen."

"Of course," Orlena replied easily. "I'd be glad to be of help. Just come with me Katie and we'll find Lloyd. Is he your sweetheart?"

"Oh no, he's my brother. My only one and I love him."

Watching the two girls stroll across the yard towards the busy, noisy corrals, Jenelle shook her head. "What has gotten into Orlena?" she wondered before hurrying back to the kitchen.

Reaching the fence, the two girls paused to lean on the gate and watch the action within. To Orlena's mind, untrained as she was in the ways and habits of ranches, all she saw before her was complete chaos. There were cows in several different corrals as well as hundreds out in the large pasture. Cowboys seemed to be everywhere, most on horseback though some were on foot. Everyone was so busy that the two girls were unnoticed.

"There he is!" Katie exclaimed, pointing to one of the corral gates. "I wonder why he isn't on Spitfire?"

"I don't know," replied Orlena. "What is he doing?" In spite of her dislike for ranch life, something about this sight drew her interest.

Katie had to speak loudly to be heard. "I think he's manning that gate. See, look, some hands are bringing another cow over to him and he's opening the gate. I wonder if they can spare him."

"Of course they can," Orlena replied. "There are plenty of other men who can open a gate. You just wait right here. I'll go fetch him." So saying, she made her way around the fence and headed over to where Lloyd was working. Before she reached him, however, she saw her brother ride up to Lloyd and heard him shout, "Shut the gate after this next cow, Hearter, and make sure it's latched. That's all we're putting in that corral this evening!"

Orlena saw Lloyd nod and watched as another cow was being herded towards the gate. Suddenly an idea of how she could get even with the young hand entered her mind. Quickly she climbed through the fence and hurried over to Lloyd who was swinging the gate open.

"Lloyd," she called.

The cow made a dash for the gate and as it entered the corral, Lloyd pushed the gate shut behind it before looking around.

"Jenelle sent me to find you and tell you that your sister is here to see you. She said that Norman would excuse you."

"Which sister?" Lloyd was skeptical.

"Katie. She just arrived home. See, there she is over by the gate. You'd better hurry, Lloyd, because she may not have much time to visit."

"Let me latch this gate and make sure it's secure first—" he began but Orlena stopped him.

"I'll latch it. Jenelle said for you to hurry."

For a moment Lloyd hesitated. He could see Katie waving to him eagerly and Mr. Mavrich hadn't given him any other instructions. Besides it was almost supper time, he hoped, and if Jenelle said to hurry . . . These thoughts flashed through his mind in an instant. "Make sure it gets latched all the way," he cautioned. "Mr. Mavrich wouldn't be one bit pleased if these cows got out!"

"I'll be very careful," Orlena promised solemnly and with that, Lloyd hurried off.

"Very careful not to latch it." Orlena smiled smugly.

CHAPTER 21

UNLATCHED GATES

"I wonder how long it will be before those stupid cows get out?" Orlena laughed to herself softly as she moved away from the noise and dust of the cattle pens towards the house. "I wish I could see Norman's face when he sees that his favorite hired hand disregarded his orders."

Once back in her own room, Orlena sat down at her small desk to start on her homework, but she was too delighted over Lloyd's upcoming trouble to concentrate. "I wonder if Norman will send him packing as soon as he notices or if he'll let him spend another night on the ranch?" Giggling, Orlena went to the window and looked out. The sun was sinking lower in the western sky and in another few hours darkness would come, but the noise of the cattle would continue all night.

The loud clang of the dinner gong sounded and Norman reined up his horse. All around the men were beginning to move towards the stables and the bunk house. Scott, Triple Creeks' wrangler, and two other men, one from the Running C and the other from the Silver Spur waited to take the tired mounts from the men. They would be the last men to eat, but on a ranch the horses were more important than dinner and their care came first.

As the men disappeared, Norman and his foreman

made a final check of the cattle and corrals. There would be no more work that evening and everything must be in shape for the night.

"Mavrich!"

Norman looked over to see Hardrich motioning to him. Quickly he rode over wondering what was up.

"What is it, Hardrich?"

"Who was in charge of this gate?" Hardrich pointed.

"Hearter was. Why? Something wrong?"

"I'll say. It isn't latched."

"What!" Norman sprang off his horse and approached the gate in question. Sure enough, it wasn't latched.

"It was a good thing I rode by it when I did," Hardrich continued, "because it was half open and one of the cows was pushing it. In another minute we would have had a fine mess on our hands."

Scowling, Norman examined the latch to see if it might have come undone by itself, but it was as sturdy as though it were new. "I don't understand it," he muttered. "I specifically told Lloyd to make sure the gate was latched."

"There must be some explanation then," Hardrich offered. "I've never known Lloyd Hearter to fail to follow instructions."

"Neither have I," Norman assented with a sigh. "But how do you explain this then?"

Neither man spoke. Both were trying to think of a plausible reason for the gate to be unlatched. Surely such a dependable hand as Lloyd wouldn't have just forgotten.

Latching the gate firmly, Norman swung back up on his horse and said, "Let's go find him and see what he says."

Hardrich nodded as he too mounted up. Then together they rode towards the bunk house. A moment later they spied the young hand standing in the yard with Jenelle and a girl. "Who's that?" the foreman asked.

Shrugging, Norman drew rein. "Don't know. But let's leave the horses. They could use a rest."

Both men swung off and approached the trio on foot.

"Hearter," Norman called as they drew near.

Lloyd turned. "Yes sir." He noticed the serious expressions on the faces of his boss and the foreman. "Is something wrong, sir?"

"Hello Mr. Mavrich, Mr. Hardrich," Katie spoke up with a smile that was slightly anxious. "I hope it was all right for Lloyd to quit work before the supper bell rang. Mrs. Mavrich said it would be all right and since it's been so long, well . . ." her voice trailed off.

"I did say that, Norman," Jenelle put in. "So don't blame Lloyd for quitting early."

"I wasn't going to. Hearter, before you left to see your sister, did you make sure the gate to the corral was latched?"

"The gate, sir? Orlena said she would latch it. She told me Mrs. Mavrich said I was to hurry. I told her to make sure it was latched all the way, and she promised she would." Suddenly Lloyd's tanned face paled. "Was the gate open, Mr. Mavrich? Did the cows—"

Hardrich shook his head. "No, the cows didn't get out, but the gate certainly wasn't latched or even shut when I checked it just a moment ago."

For a brief moment, Lloyd stared at the foreman then he groaned. "I should have known better than to trust her."

Light steps were heard approaching them and everyone looked up to see Orlena. She would have passed them with scarcely a nod, but her brother stopped her.

"Orlena, step over here a minute, please."

"Yes?" Orlena queried in haughty politeness.

"Did you latch the gate to the corral after you talked with Lloyd?"

"Of course not, why should I? It's not my job."

"He said you promised to latch it for him so he could hurry to see his sister," Norman's voice was low.

"Well, I like that!" exclaimed Orlena indignantly. "I told him that his sister was waiting to speak with him and then asked him if the gate was supposed to be latched before he left. He told me it was none of my business and left."

"Why didn't you find Mr. Hardrich or myself and ask about it?" Norman questioned.

Snorting, Orlena gave her brother a look of disgust. "You expected me to tramp through that mob of filthy cattle just to ask if a gate was supposed to be latched? You are dumb."

During this exchange, Lloyd's hands clenched at his sides and his face flushed. He knew nothing like that had happened, but what could he say except repeat the truth?

After eyeing his sister for several long seconds, Norman, who had been thinking hard, turned suddenly to Katie. "Miss Katie," he asked, "did you go with Orlena to find your brother?"

Katie shook her head. "Only as far as the first gate, Mr. Mavrich. If I had gone all the way, we would probably still be standing at that gate."

"Hearter, what were you doing when Orlena first spoke to you?"

There was a brief moment of silence before Lloyd replied, "I was lettin' that last cow in, sir."

"I see. Orlena, why did you ask if the gate was supposed to be latched?" This question seemed to the others to be rather obvious, for if a gate wasn't latched, the cattle or whatever was behind it could easily open it. However, Norman waited silently for Orlena to answer.

"Aren't all gates supposed to be latched?"

"How did you know we weren't putting any other cattle in that corral?"

"I heard you say something to him about the last one as I came up. Why?"

"I just wondered." Norman was looking at her closely, and she flushed under his steady gaze. "Hearter," Norman turned to the young hand who had remained silent. "Are you sure Orlena told you she would latch the gate?"

"Yes, Sir!" Lloyd was emphatic. "She said she would latch the gate because Mrs. Mavrich wanted me to hurry."

"Was anyone else around, Hearter?" The foreman

asked the question in hopes that someone else might have overheard the conversation.

"Not that I remember noticing, sir."

"Well!" Orlena exclaimed with a toss of her head. "It looks like it is my word against that of a mere hired hand. It shouldn't take even a college graduate long to know who is speaking the truth."

There was a flash in the eyes of the owner of the Triple Creek Ranch at his sister's words. He was convinced in his own mind about the event but all he said was, "We won't go into it any more. Just make sure all the gates are latched before you leave them, Hearter."

"Yes, Sir."

Clasping him gently on the shoulder, Norman smiled briefly at his hand before turning away.

"Norman," Jenelle's soft voice called him back. "I know it's getting later, but couldn't Lloyd ride back to town with Katie and eat supper with his family tonight since Katie has just gotten home? It really is getting too late for Katie to be out riding alone."

Briefly Norman nodded. "Ride Minuet, Lloyd. She needs the exercise and Spitfire needs a longer rest. Spend the night if you want, just make sure you're here in time for morning chores."

"Oh, thank you, Mr. Mavrich, Mrs. Mavrich!" Katie exclaimed in delight. "Mother will be so pleased to see him." Then she hurried away to find her brother who was already saddling up Minuet.

Telling his wife he would be with her in a minute, Norman stepped away for a few low words with his foreman. "I'm sure Hearter is telling the truth. My sister probably did say she would latch the gate but never intended to. Ever since that first day she was here, when Lloyd stopped her from striking Minuet, she's had a grudge against him." Hardrich nodded and Norman continued. "I don't know if she'll try anything else, but let's keep this thing quiet."

"That why you sent Lloyd off?"

Norman grinned. "Yep. But with his character, I'd trust him with everything I've got and not worry."

Agreeing emphatically, Hardrich added, "He certainly has the right character."

"Now let's go get some dinner. I'm hungry clear through to my backbone." And Norman hurried off to join Jenelle who had waited for him.

That night, in the solitude of her room, Orlena paced the floor in anger. Why didn't Norman believe her word against the word of a hired hand? How could she get Lloyd Hearter fired from the ranch? There must be some way. There had to be! He couldn't be as perfect as he appeared. Surely he would slip up on something, and if he did, she would be ready. At last Orlena went to bed, still trying to create a plan that would bring about Lloyd's dismissal from the Triple Creek Ranch.

T

The long days of sorting cattle continued and still Orlena could come up with nothing against Lloyd Hearter. This fact made her more irritable than before and she grumbled and fussed about anything she was asked to do. Jenelle was thankful that Norman was too busy to notice his sister's attitude.

"I don't know what to do with her any longer, Mrs. O'Connor," Jenelle confided to the older woman one morning after Orlena had left for school. "I don't know which is more tiring, her earlier haughty attitude with furious bursts of temper now and then and her self-pity or now when every word she utters is a complaint or anger."

"Aye, 'tis a hard life Miss Orlena is leading surely," Mrs. O'Connor agreed. "And it's often I'm a wonderin' what it will take before the Good Lord has her for His own. 'Tis not like to be an easy way."

Jenelle sighed. "No, it isn't going to be easy for anyone." A few moments of silence passed before Jenelle, with a complete change of tone and manner asked, "Mrs. O'Connor, what do you think of ranch life now?"

"Think of it? To tell you the truth, I'm enjoyin' it entirely."

"Good, I was hoping you were because I don't know what I would do without you now." And Jenelle smiled brightly on her housekeeper and friend.

"Hearter," Norman called above the noise of many voices as he beckoned. Supper was just finished in the large bunk house and the men were relaxing as they talked about the day.

Lloyd made his way through the crowd of cattlemen to where his boss was waiting with Mrs. Mavrich, Orlena and Mrs. O'Connor before retiring to the ranch house for the night. "You called me, Sir?"

"Yes. Tompkins says there's going to be a storm tonight, and you know he's never wrong. I want you to go out and check the corrals."

"Make sure things are shut tight. The last thing we need is a stampede the night before we drive them to the stockyards. Everything should be fine, but I don't want to take any chances."

Lloyd nodded. "Sure thing, Boss. I'll head out there now before it grows completely dark. Good night, Sir, Mrs. Mavrich, Mrs. O'Connor," he nodded to each one as he spoke before turning, catching up his hat and hurrying away.

"Good night, Lloyd," Mrs. Mavrich called after him pleasantly.

"Norman!" Orlena exclaimed suddenly. "Is it starting to grow dark?"

"I reckon," he sighed, too tired to wonder at his sister's question.

"Then I'm leaving right now. I haven't taken care of the chickens yet."

"That should have been done before you ate," her brother growled in disgust.

Orlena didn't give him an answer but hurried away. However, had anyone been watching, they would have wondered why she turned towards the large corrals when the chicken house was the other direction. If the truth were told, Orlena had already taken care of the chickens, for her horror of the dark out in the middle of the country was too great to leave them until late. In reality, an idea had just occurred to her which might send the one person she heartily disliked away from the ranch forever.

Keeping out of sight, Orlena crept along in the shadows watching as Lloyd checked each gate with care, while he whistled a tune of his own making. After making sure everything was latched tightly, Lloyd turned and retraced his steps to the bunk house, Orlena watching with glee. As soon as he was gone, she hurried around to the first corral and slid back the latch. Hesitating a moment, she thought of opening the gate and trying to get the cattle out, but realized that would take too long. The twilight was settling quickly into the gloom of evening and with a shiver she quickly moved to the second corral. Not daring to remain out any longer, Orlena dashed to the barn and then to the house arriving slightly out of breath.

Norman looked up as Orlena entered the kitchen. "What's the trouble?" he asked.

"Nothing. I just don't like the dark out there," Orlena shivered.

"If you'd take care of your responsibilities before supper like you are supposed to, you wouldn't have to be out in the dark," Norman commented dryly.

"And if I had a brother with any feelings at all, I wouldn't have to be doing such belittling things as taking care of a bunch of chickens!" snapped Orlena.

Instead of answering, Norman turned and walked out of the room. He was too tired to get into an argument with his sister then. All he wanted was a bed.

It was late. All was quiet on the Triple Creek Ranch save for the mournful bawling of the cattle separated in different corrals. The inmates of both the bunk house and the ranch house were sleeping soundly, most of them exhausted by the long, hard days and weeks they had spent. Every cattleman, Jim Hardrich and Norman Mavrich included, had sunk into heavy slumber with the sense of near accomplishment; tomorrow was the day to drive the cattle to the train station and then all the extra hands, borrowed for the round-up, would head back to their respected ranches and life would take on a slower pace for a time.

Suddenly the quietness of sleep was shattered, for all at once a bolt of lightning sliced through the heavens with a blinding light which lit up the entire sky, followed almost instantly by a terrific explosion of thunder which shook every structure on the ranch as it rolled on and on, bouncing off the hills, echoing in the valleys and seeming to fill everything with its sound. Simultaneously with the thunder, Norman was out of his bed and throwing on his clothes.

CHAPTER 22

UNEXPECTED RESULTS

"Norman, what are you doing?" Jenelle exclaimed, sitting up as the house seemed to quiver in sound.

"The cattle stampede in this kind of weather."

"But Lloyd checked the gates."

"I'm just checking." Before Jenelle could say another word, Norman was out of the room and dashing down the stairs.

Hurriedly Jenelle threw a warm wrap about her and followed. In the hall she met Mrs. O'Connor.

"What is the excitement?" she asked.

"Norman's gone to check on the cattle," Jenelle said, trying not to sound worried.

"In this weather? Has the boy gone daft? 'Tis not a night to be out with cattle I'll be certain. But, come, if yer a mind to and we'll wait for the man downstairs. 'Tis likely he'll be wantin' some hot coffee when he comes in drenched to the bone."

Jenelle nodded and the two women made their way to the kitchen where lamps were lighted and the coffee put on.

Meanwhile, Norman, having slapped his hat on his head as he dashed out the door, raced towards the corrals. The storm hadn't let loose yet, but he expected a downpour at any moment. "What!" he exclaimed in dismay, as the sight of cattle running out of two of the corrals and milling in fright with the others in the larger pen met his eyes. Wheeling quickly, he dashed to the bunk house and flung open the door. "Hurry men!" he shouted. "Get your horses! We've got the start of a stampede out there and at least two of the corrals are open! Let's go!"

Before he had finished, every man was out of his bed and on his feet, pulling on his clothes in record time, slapping hats on their heads and shoving their feet into their boots. Had they been racing to a fire they couldn't have made better time, for each man knew what a stampede could mean to a ranch and, with at least two corrals open, perhaps the others were open as well and all their work would have to be done over.

Another rumble of thunder, not as startling as the first one, sounded as the men dashed from the bunk house to the stables where the horses, as though sensing things were not right, were moving about restlessly.

Finding Norman ready to mount his dependable mustang, Hardrich paused briefly to ask, "What happened?"

Norman shook his head. "I don't know. We'll find out later. Right now we've got to get the cattle under control."

"Here's your mount, Mr. Hardrich," Scott's voice broke in.

"Thanks." The foreman sprang up and turned the horse's head.

"I'll take the first ten men," Norman called, "We'll start trying to circle the cattle. When you get a group, head over to the other corrals and check them!"

"Got it," Hardrich shouted back.

As Norman dashed from the stables, Lloyd, Alden, Tompkins and St. John of the Triple Creek were right behind him along with six others from different ranches. No one had to be told what to do. They all knew. Stopping a stampede was dangerous work especially in a storm, for when the ground became wet it grew slick and the chance of horses or cattle slipping in the mud were great, yet not one of the men hesitated. It was all part of the job.

The rain hadn't begun yet as Norman led his men into the midst of the terror stricken mob of cattle. "Turn 'em right!" he shouted. "We'll—" the rest of his sentence was cut off by another clap of thunder and then the heavens opened and the rain came down in buckets. After that it was hard to see except when the jagged forks of lightning raced across the sky and even then the light was so fleeting that it would have been easier had there been no light at all.

Hardrich and a handful of men headed over to the corrals and, besides the two which were open and empty, they found them shut securely. The other men had joined the rest in trying to get the herd of cattle to circle. All was confusion, cattle were trying to run in any and every direction spooked by the startling flashes of light, only to be turned back by men on horseback who shouted and blocked their way. The ground, so dusty and dry during the day, now became a sea of wet, slippery mud as the many hooves stirred it up while the steady downpour continued. Several cows slipped and wallowed in the mire until they regained their feet once again. Even a few horses were slipping when they tried to turn too quickly.

Five minutes passed in total confusion. Then ten. At last Norman and a few other hands managed to turn the leading cattle to the right and start them in a circle. There was still plenty of danger, for though most of the cattle were turned, there were still others on the outskirts of the mob who could start the herd off again. Every sense was alert, every muscle tensed for split second reaction, every eye straining to see into the falling rain and hear the calls of the other men over the rumble of almost continual thunder.

In the ranch house, Mrs. Mavrich and Mrs. O'Connor waited. Jenelle had been pacing the floor and suddenly turned to the older woman. "I have to go out and find Norman!"

"Jenelle Mavrich, you'll do no such thing," exclaimed Mrs. O'Connor emphatically. "'Twould be a fine thing indeed if Norman were to come back to find his wife missing on such a night like this."

"But where is he?"

"Most likely he's waiting the rain out in the bunk house or one of the outbuildings. I wouldn't fret, Child. My mother always used to be tellin' me that if I was worried, 'twas a sure sign I should be doin' some prayin'."

Standing by the window, Jenelle remained silent for a moment, trying to pierce the darkness with her eyes in hopes of seeing her husband returning. She knew only too well the dangers that could come when cattle, storms and cowboys mix. At last she spoke, "Help me to pray, Mrs. O'Connor. I don't know why, but I feel as though something isn't right."

Mrs. O'Connor smiled gently at the young mistress of the ranch. "Of course, Jenelle. Let us kneel down right here. Remember, where two or three are gathered . . ."

"There am I in the midst," Jenelle finished. "Oh, Mrs. O'Connor, how I wish Orlena was one with us!"

"That will come. I feel sure of it."

Then together the two women knelt in prayer for Norman's safety and for the safety of any others who might be out in the storm.

The ticking of the old clock in the room, the drumming of rain and the now occasional rumble of thunder were the only sounds. Mrs. O'Connor sat at the table, a cup of tea before her. At the window, Jenelle stood, silent and still, watching for any sign of movement out in the darkness.

Suddenly she gave a slight cry and hurried to the door. Flinging it wide open she held her wrap close about her as the wind blew the chilling rain into her face and called, "Lloyd!"

A dim form appeared out of the darkness and a voice called, "Mrs. Mavrich!" It wasn't Lloyd.

"Alden," Jenelle exclaimed as the exhausted hand came closer, "I thought I saw Lloyd. What are you doing? Where's Norman? What's happened?" This last she added in a frightened tone, for by the light of the kitchen lamp she could now see the hired hand's pale face. "Tell me, Alden, what happened?"

"It's Mr. Mavrich, Ma'am. Lloyd's gone for the doctor. He took Minuet. His horse was too played out."

Jenelle gave a startled gasp and pressed her hands over her heart. For a moment she felt lightheaded and dazed. Was this a dream? What she had feared had happened. Norman had been hurt!

Mrs. O'Connor's calm voice roused her. "Are they bringing him here?" she asked.

"Yes, Ma'am. Hardrich sent me ahead to . . ." he hesitated. "To let Mrs. Mavrich know."

"Alden," Jenelle whispered, "Norman isn't— isn't . . ." She couldn't say the word.

"No ma'am. He's unconscious and I ain't sure how bad he's hurt, but he's still breathin'," Alden assured her quickly.

"Thank God!"

"If they're bringing him here, we had best get ready to receive them. Jenelle, go up and get the bed ready. Alden, fill that kettle and put it on to boil. I'll go get some extra blankets and some bandages. Let's fly around now."

When Norman Mavrich was brought in several minutes later, carried tenderly on a makeshift stretcher by his own foreman and hired hands, they were ready for him. With great gentleness he was borne upstairs and placed upon his own bed which he had left in such a hurry only a few hours before.

Jenelle, with a face almost as pale as that of her husband, knelt beside his still form with one small hand holding his limp one and the other gently smoothing back his wet hair. For some time she remained thus, watching each breath her husband took, then, at last, when weariness began to creep over her, she laid her face on the pillow beside him. Not one word did she utter and not a sound came from her trembling lips after the first half strangled cry which had escaped when he was first brought in. She didn't ask what happened nor did she seem to notice anyone until a hand was placed on her shoulder and she raised her eyes to see Dr. French beside her.

Orlena had been awakened from her sleep by the tramping of many booted feet on the stairs. Not a little startled by these unusual sounds, she crept from her bed and tiptoed to the door of her room which she opened just a little and peered out into the hall. There were lights on in Norman and Jenelle's room as well as in the hall. She could see but little, and though she listened hard, could hear even less. At last the footsteps returned and Orlena could see the men of Triple Creek Ranch moving from the bedroom and slowly making their way down the stairs. All were silent and tried to tread the hall and stairs as softly as possible.

A sudden fear seized Orlena Mavrich then, a fear that crept quickly through her entire being and which set her heart to pounding and her pulse racing. What could have happened? That something dreadful had occurred, she was quite certain. The lights were still on in the bedroom though the door was shut. Could it be that Jenelle was sick? If that were so, why were the hired hands in the house? Perhaps Norman was sick. But then they would have sent for the doctor and not the hands. She had not heard Norman leave the house after the first startling clap of thunder, so no thought of anyone being injured crossed her mind. Instead of getting up as the rest of the family had done when roused by the storm, she had simply pulled the pillow over her head and gone back to sleep, completely forgetting about those unlatched corrals.

At last, with a desperate fear tugging at her heart, she slipped from her room into the hallway. There she hesitated. Should she, dare she, push open the bedroom door and see for herself what was wrong? Reaching out her hand, she touched the door and then drew back. No, she couldn't open that door. Swiftly turning, she moved to the stairs and, on seeing the lights downstairs, glided down, her bare feet making no noise.

The men gathered in groups talking in hushed voices turned as the white figure entered and asked in frightened tones, "What's happening?"

For a moment no one answered, then St. John stepped over to her and replied quietly, "Your brother has been hurt. Mrs. Mavrich, Mrs. O'Connor and Mr. Hardrich are with him now."

"Hurt?" Orlena turned puzzled eyes on the speaker. "How did he get hurt? Why are you all here and so wet and muddy? Where's the doctor? What time is it?" Her voice was rising almost hysterically. "What happened?"

"Shh," St. John warned. "Keep your voice quiet so you don't disturb him. Here, sit down, and we'll tell you." He pulled out a chair and Orlena, still dazed and frightened, obeyed.

"Lloyd's gone for the doctor. There was a stampede of cattle caused by the storm. Two of the corrals came open and when Mr. Mavrich went to check on them it was a fine mess."

"The corrals were open?"

"Thankfully only two," Alden put in. "If the rest had been open we really would have had trouble and the casualties would have been worse."

"Was Norman the only one to get . . . hurt?" Orlena hesitated and clasped her hands tightly together.

"No, one of the men from the Silver Spur has some nasty wire cuts from his horse slipping and spilling him into the fence. Then too, Scott has what appears to be some busted ribs."

This news was not comforting and Orlena wished she had stayed in bed. But she had to know everything now that she knew some. "But what happened? How did Norman get hurt? And why was he outside in the storm?" she persisted.

"He was out checkin' the cattle. With a storm the size we got, there could have been trouble even if the corrals hadn't been open."

"Why weren't you with him?" accused Orlena.

"We were. He was in the middle of the cattle," St. John began, "when his horse slipped or was knocked down by some frightened cows. No one is quite sure what happened. When we got to him he was unconscious. It's a miracle he wasn't killed!"

T

CHAPTER 23

WAITING

Orlena's face paled. For the first time she realized that her brother wasn't just lying up in bed with a few cuts and bruises. He could have been, should have been, dead! She shuddered. Dead. He was her only living family and if he— Shaking her head she looked about the room almost wildly. "Where is the doctor?" she demanded, springing to her feet. "Why isn't he here? Doesn't he know that Norman Mavrich is lying up in his room badly hurt? Why are you all just standing there? Go bring him!"

Quiet steps sounded on the stairs and Jim Hardrich entered. Going over to Orlena he caught her shoulders and turned her around. In tones of quiet authority he spoke. "Calm down, Orlena. Getting excited won't bring the doctor any quicker. Lloyd has taken the fastest horse and gone for him. I know it's hardest of all to wait, but there isn't a thing we can do for him except to pray."

Looking up into the lined, weather beaten face of the older foreman, Orlena felt a sense of calm assurance, as though things would be all right. Then, as he bowed his head and began to pray, she glanced around and noticed that every head in the room was bowed. As she listened to the prayers of the men for their boss and fellow hands, unexpected tears welled up in the girl's eyes. Suddenly she began to get a dim idea of how much her brother meant to these "mere hired hands."

At last the door opened and the doctor entered and took off his dripping hat and jacket.

"I'll see to your horse, Doc," Gregory said, hurrying from the house while Hardrich led the doctor upstairs to the bedroom where Norman still lay unconscious.

It was over an hour before the doctor descended the stairs with Mr. Hardrich. To those waiting below it seemed like days.

"How is he?" Alden asked anxiously.

"Still unconscious. He's got a couple busted ribs, and a broken leg, besides being pretty beat up. When he'll wake up, I don't know. Hardrich," Dr. French turned to the foreman, "can one of the men remain up there in the hall or someplace close by while I'm seeing to the other men, in case I'm needed?"

"Sure thing, Doc. St. John, will you take the watch?"

St. John nodded and silently disappeared upstairs.

Having slipped his jacket on, for though the rain had all but stopped, the air was brisk and chilly, the doctor turned, but before he could leave he caught a glimpse of Orlena in her white nightgown, curled up in a chair hugging her knees. His face grew gentle. "As for you, Miss Orlena, why don't you head up to bed. We'll wake you if anything happens."

Stubbornly she shook her head. "I'm staying here."

Shrugging, Dr. French followed Hardrich outside to the bunkhouse with Alden, Gregory and Smith trailing behind.

Left alone, Orlena soon became chilled and, going into the front room, curled up on the sofa with a quilt about her. For several minutes she lay there thinking and imagining what would happen if her brother were to die. Not once did the thought that she was at least partially responsible for her brother's injuries come to her. "Perhaps Norman won't want to stay on the ranch any longer after he gets well. He could just let his foreman run it and he could move to the city." She yawned and settled a little more comfortably among the pillows. She wasn't going to sleep, she wanted to stay awake until Norman woke up, for she was sure it wouldn't be long. However, after a second yawn, her eyes closed and she slept.

Upstairs in the bedroom where Norman lay still and motionless except for his breathing, there was no sleeping. Jenelle had been settled in her rocking chair close beside the bed where she could watch her husband's face. Mrs. O'Connor, who was a capable nurse, followed the doctor's directions and stepped softly about the room before establishing herself in a straight-backed chair where she could also keep watch. Outside in the hallway, St. John sat on a chair and waited and prayed.

After a while, having taped Scott's broken ribs and bandaged the wire cuts on the other cowhand, Dr. French returned to the house, leaving Hardrich and the other hands to get some needed sleep.

"I'll send St. John out to you if there is any change," he promised. "Oh, and don't wait up for Lloyd. That horse he was riding was all done in when he reached my place. I told him to bed her down in my stable, and my wife fixed him a place to sleep in the house. He'll be back in the morning though, I reckon."

Hardrich nodded and in silence watched the doctor hurry back across the yard. Then his gaze moved to the now quiet pasture and corrals. Shaking his head, he let out a long sigh and shut the door. "How did those corrals get opened?" he wondered tiredly as he sat down on his bed and pulled off his boots. "Lloyd checked them." Wearily he stretched out and pulled up the blanket. "And I checked them all before coming in for supper. I just know he wouldn't have opened them. But if he didn't, then who did?" Unable to answer that question, Triple Creek's foreman whispered another prayer for Norman, turned over and fell asleep.

When morning dawned and the sun rose, it found stirring in the bunkhouse as the men prepared to do their work over again and sort out the cattle one more time. They were just thankful that the other corrals hadn't been open. All wondered how Mr. Mavrich was, for St. John had brought them no news during the night.

Hardrich sent Scott over to the ranch house to relieve the ranch hand's cook. "Since you won't be riding today anyhow, you can remain over there."

When he arrived at the bunk house, St. John reported no change. Mr. Mavrich was still unconscious.

"How's Mrs. Mavrich?" Hardrich questioned.

St. John shrugged. "I don't know. She hasn't left his side all night. Mrs. O'Connor went and got an hour or two of sleep."

"And Orlena?"

Scratching his chin in puzzlement, St. John shook his head, "I haven't seen her since I went up last night. I wonder where she is?" Then, after a pause he asked, "You don't think she ran away, do you?"

Surprised by the question, Hardrich turned back to the cook. "Now why would she do that?"

St. John gave another shrug. "It was just a thought that crossed my mind, since I ain't seen her."

"Well, don't spread it around," the foreman ordered. "We've got enough trouble without borrowing more."

While the men were finishing their breakfast, the door was suddenly flung open and Lloyd appeared. "How's the boss?"

Hardrich shook his head. "Still unconscious. A couple broken ribs and a busted leg."

With a groan Lloyd's hands clenched and he pounded one fist against the doorframe. "I was sure they were latched when I checked them! It's my fault!"

"Easy, Hearter, no one is blaming you." Jim Hardrich rose and placed a hand on the young, agitated man's shoulder. "Suppose you sit down and have some breakfast."

"I'm not hungry." He turned away. "Besides, I have to

take care of Minuet. I'll meet you all at the corrals." His voice was low and subdued.

"Hardrich," Alden asked as the foreman continued to stand and watch the retreating form of the young hand. "Who did open those gates?"

"I don't know, Alden. I just don't know." Then his voice changed. "Come on men, we've got work to do if we're going to get these cattle to the stock yards before tomorrow's train."

Orlena, upon awakening and finding herself not in her own room, lay for several minutes looking about her and trying to recall why she had been sleeping in the front room. Suddenly it all came back to her and she started up. Had anything happened while she slept? The doctor had promised to tell her, but had he known where she was?

Quickly and silently she slipped upstairs to her own room. Scott saw her, and in answer to her anxious look, shook his head. "No change."

Almost without thinking, Orlena made ready for school. She gathered her books and, carrying her shoes, slipped back out into the silent hallway. In the dining room she put on her shoes.

The door opened and Alden entered. Upon seeing Orlena, he paused and said in hushed tones, "St. John has breakfast made in the bunkhouse."

"I'm not hungry."

Alden looked troubled. "You aren't going to school without eating, are you? Has there been a change in Mr. Mavrich?"

Orlena looked up and snapped, "No! And I said I wasn't hungry!" With that she snatched up her books and rushed from the house, leaving the hired hand looking after her with surprise, bewilderment and concern.

Returning home after school, Orlena discovered there was no change in her brother's condition. Pensively she did her chores and restlessly wandered about the yard. She watched the men return from the cattle pens, hot, tired, muddy, full of concern for the master of the ranch, yet more than ready to fill up on St. John's cooking. Idly Orlena wondered if she was expected to eat in the bunk house with the hired hands or if Mrs. O'Connor would come down from the sick room long enough to prepare supper for those of the house.

Less than ten minutes later, Mr. Hardrich approached her. "Orlena, I'm afraid you will have to eat at the bunk house tonight, for Mrs. O'Connor hasn't time to cook now."

Orlena sniffed. "Oh indeed. What is she doing that prevents her from doing her work?"

The ranch foreman replied quietly, "She's needed in your brother's sick room."

"And what of Jenelle? If Mrs. O'Connor is too busy, surely Jenelle could—"

"Your sister won't leave Mr. Mavrich."

Feelings of frustration that all her plans were failing, Orlena stamped her foot and pouted. "How can someone who isn't even doing anything need so much attention?" she demanded crossly.

Hardrich smiled. "I can't answer that. Save that question for the doctor. Now supper's ready. St. John won't ring the bell tonight."

For a minute Orlena remained where she was, motionless, trying to decide if she would go to the bunk house of her own free will and eat with the hired hands or not. She knew she couldn't openly say she didn't eat with hired help anymore for she had eaten with them several times. It wasn't the food that she disapproved of either, for she had to admit that St. John's cooking was among the best she had ever eaten, it was just the company.

Standing up from the wooden bench she had been sitting on, Orlena suddenly felt lightheaded and slightly dizzy. Turning towards the house, she said, "I . . . I don't feel like eating." She swayed as she spoke and Hardrich, springing to her side, caught her as she fell.

"Just what we need," he muttered, carrying the limp form into the house. "Norman still unconscious, Mrs. Mavrich not wanting to eat or leave him and now this."

Dr. French met him in the hall as he came up the steps with his light burden. "What's this?" he asked sharply.

Hardrich shook his head. "She fainted just now. I'll carry her to her room."

Mrs. O'Connor was quietly called and Orlena was placed on her bed. There the doctor bent over the quiet form and frowned as he applied restoratives.

"Where was this child today?"

Hardrich shrugged and Mrs. O'Connor replied, "Scott said she went to school."

"Did she eat breakfast before she left?"

It was Hardrich's turn to shake his head. "St. John said she never came in."

"Humph," Dr. French snorted with a shake of his head. "And I suppose she didn't take anything to eat at noon then either."

No one could answer that question but in another minute Orlena's eyes opened.

For a moment she lay in silence, her eyes moving slowly from one face to another as though asking what had happened, then without a word she turned her face away.

"What this child needs is a good meal," the doctor said. "Hardrich, see if you can't rustle up some grub for her."

The foreman nodded. "Be right back."

"I'm not hungry." The low spoken words came from the bed.

Dr. French paid no heed to them, instead he turned to Mrs. O'Connor. "Before her supper arrives, Mrs. O'Connor, she should have a glass of milk. Can you bring that about?"

"To be sure, Doctor." And Mrs. O'Connor quietly left the room.

"I said I wasn't hungry," persisted Orlena in a louder voice.

Drawing a chair up beside the bed, Dr. French sat down. "Now see here, young lady," he began kindly but firmly, "your not eating is what has caused this commotion in the first place. I know you don't feel like eating with your brother sick, but the best thing you can do for him right now is to eat and remain on your feet. You don't want to worry your sister and cause more trouble for Mrs. O'Connor."

"But I don't want to eat," Orlena pouted. "Why do I have to?"

"Let's just say because the doctor ordered it," was the unsatisfactory reply as Mrs. O'Connor opened the door carrying a glass of milk.

It was late at night. Everything on the ranch was quiet. Mrs. O'Connor was sleeping in her room while the doctor kept watch in the sickroom. Also in the room, where a dim light burned, Jenelle sat in her rocking chair close beside the bed. She didn't sleep or even close her eyes. There she had remained, in spite of pleadings from Mrs. O'Connor, Dr. French and even Hardrich and young Lloyd. Very quietly and steadily she had refused to heed their words; often it appeared as though she didn't even hear them, for her eyes never left her husband's face. It was only when the doctor told her firmly that she must eat if she wanted to keep up her strength, that she was persuaded to partake of the food Mrs. O'Connor brought her.

Everything was quiet and still. The crickets had ceased their nightly concert, and even the leaves on the trees seemed to hang in slumber outside the windows as though tired from dancing to the songs of the night orchestra. Jenelle, in her rocker, sat and prayed as the hours slowly slipped away. Suddenly she straightened and leaned forward. A slight sound had come from the still form on the bed.

℃

CHAPTER 24

A MATTER OF CHATACTER

Trying to draw a deep breath, the pain from his broken ribs brought a low moan to Norman's lips and his eyes opened slowly.

Scarcely daring to move or breathe, Jenelle watched. Was she dreaming? Had Norman regained consciousness?

Another groan came from the bed as Norman turned his head a little. Then came a whisper, "Jenelle?"

Instantly Jenelle was beside the bed bending over him, one hand in his, gently smoothing his hair with the other, and smiling. "I'm here, Darling," she replied quietly, her eyes filling with unshed tears.

Blinking in a bewildered way, Norman inquired feebly, "What happened? What time is it?"

After a quick glance at the doctor who had risen unnoticed and was standing nearby, and seeing his nod, Jenelle answered softly, "There was an accident and you were hurt. But it's late, Dear, and you should be sleeping. Swallow this for me and then get some sleep please." And she held a spoon to his lips.

With a slight smile, Norman did as he was bid, but whispered, "Aren't you coming to bed?"

"Soon, Darling, soon," Jenelle soothed. "Now sleep."

His eyes closed once more and moments later his steady breathing told the watchers that he was asleep. Softly

Jenelle placed a kiss on his forehead and then looked anxiously at the doctor who had his fingers on Norman's pulse.

Giving a satisfied nod, Dr. French inclined his head towards the door and Jenelle, sliding her hand from Norman's relaxed hold, followed with soft tread. Out in the hall, with the door of the room closed behind them, the doctor smiled. "I think he'll be all right now, Mrs. Mavrich."

"Oh, thank God!" breathed Jenelle, clasping her hands.

"Yes indeed. Now," the doctor continued in business like tones. "You must get some rest."

Before Jenelle could protest, for her singing heart felt as though she could stay up the rest of the night as well as not, Mrs. O'Connor appeared beside them and heard the news. Immediately she took charge. "Then Doctor, just you be going back and staying with Norman 'till I return. 'Tis only to be seeing Jenelle to bed that I'll be gone surely. Then you can rest and I'll be staying with him entirely."

Dr. French smiled and nodded his approval before slipping back to the sick room. He enjoyed Mrs. O'Connor's refreshing nursing skills and her way of handling situations.

Though Jenelle protested to Mrs. O'Connor that she was not tired and knew she wouldn't be able to sleep even if she were to lie down, she complied with the housekeeper's request that she try it, and no sooner did her head touch the pillow than she was deep in the land of slumbers.

"For so He giveth his beloved sleep," thought the old Irish woman as she drew a blanket over Jenelle's sleeping figure.

Turning from the bed, her eyes caught sight of the bunk house. Instantly she wondered if there were any lying awake out there wondering and worrying over Norman. She quietly hurried to the sick room and whispered a few words to the doctor who nodded and rose at once.

The bunk house was dark and still, but Lloyd Hearter couldn't sleep. For hours he had tossed and turned, but still sleep wouldn't come. Every time he closed his eyes he could see the accident. At last he rose and quietly pulling on his clothes, moved on stocking feet into the dining room and opened the outside door. There he stood drawing in deep breaths of the cool night air. He didn't know how long he stood there when a sudden hand on his shoulder startled him.

Turning quickly, he saw the foreman behind him.

"Didn't mean to startle you, Hearter," he said. "Couldn't you sleep?"

Lloyd shook his head. "No, sir. I keep thinking about those gates and Mr. Mavrich. I know they were latched when I checked them, sir. I know it, yet—"

"Hold it, Son," Jim Hardrich halted the flow of words. "I believe you. I checked them myself before heading in to eat, and they were latched. And I know you wouldn't have opened them."

"No sir! But . . ." wearily Lloyd leaned against the doorframe. "The question is, will Mr. Mavrich believe me if he wakes up."

"Stop that kind of talk, Hearter. You are letting your mind run away with your common sense. Of course Norman Mavrich will believe you. You know he isn't a man to accuse anyone without proof."

"Aren't his injuries proof enough? Someone had to open them and I was the last one near them!"

"Lloyd, your character is going to be the only proof Mr. Mavrich needs to know you weren't responsible for last night's accident."

The young man didn't answer for some time, but the slight trembling of his shoulders told the foreman that all the emotions of the last twenty-four hours were taking their toll. Reaching out, he firmly squeezed Lloyd's shoulders in silent sympathy.

Through the darkness, from the main house, a figure was seen approaching quickly. Jim Hardrich steeled himself for bad news when he recognized the form of the doctor.

"What is it?" he asked as Dr. French came close. "Has

something happened?"

"Mavrich woke up. I think he'll be all right. He's sleeping now."

"Thank God!" Lloyd and Hardrich exclaimed simultaneously. And Lloyd added, "How's Mrs. Mavrich, Doc?"

"She's sleeping. Mrs. O'Connor is watching Norman now, and I'd better get back and get some shut eye myself before morning." He turned to go, but paused and looked back as he added, "And I would recommend that you two men do the same."

As the doctor's retreating form grew dark, Hardrich pulled Lloyd inside and shut the door. "We'd better get some sleep now if we're going to drive the cattle to the stockyards in the morning." When no reply came from his younger companion, the foreman said, "Now forget all about gates and stampedes. You can talk the whole thing over with Mr. Mavrich as soon as the doctor gives you leave. Right now forget it. That's an order."

"Yes, sir," Lloyd replied quietly, and after breathing a prayer of thanksgiving, was soon sleeping.

"You're not getting up, Norman," Jenelle insisted, both small hands on her husband's shoulders. "You can't go out and see the cattle or talk with the hands. You have to rest."

Wincing slightly, Norman allowed himself to be gently forced back among the pillows. "Well," he grumbled good naturedly, "if you won't let me out, send Hardrich in to talk to me."

"Sorry, I can't do it."

"Why not? he demanded.

"Because he isn't here right now," and Jenelle rose to shut the blinds. It was mid afternoon and Jenelle was trying to get her husband to relax and sleep after his lunch which Mrs. O'Connor had just carried away.

"Where is he? Oh, Jenelle, don't shut the blinds," he begged. "I don't want to sleep."

With a smile Jenelle adjusted the last shade and turned back to the bed. "Norman Mavrich," she chided gently, "you heard what the doctor said. Sleep today and tomorrow you can talk. Now I won't answer another question until you've had a nap. Hush," she placed her fingers over his lips as he seemed ready to speak again.

Reaching up, Norman caught her hand and placed a kiss on the fingers, then drawing a deep breath which turned into a moan as his taped ribs protested, he obediently closed his eyes.

After seeing him asleep, Jenelle softly left the room and descending the stairs, sank onto a chair in the kitchen. "Oh, Mrs. O'Connor," she sighed, "what would we have done without you?"

"That's a question ye'll not be likely to answer entirely, so tis not worth thinkin' over I'm sure," replied that good woman as she finished drying the dishes. "Is Norman sleeping?"

"Yes."

"Then you go lie down for a spell, sure and twill do ye good," she added as Jenelle shook her head. "And why not?"

"I didn't help at all yesterday with the housework and—"

"And it's not likely I'll be needing any help today either. So go along."

With another sigh and a half concealed yawn, Jenelle rose and slowly made her way back up the stairs to the spare room. Her mind was too tired to do much thinking but as she lay down on the bed, she realized that she hadn't talked with Orlena or even seen her since the accident. "The poor girl," she thought. "I've been so focused on Norman that I forgot all about her. I'll try to make it up to her when she gets home from school. I wonder . . ." She never knew what she wondered for her eyes closed of themselves and she too was asleep.

The promised talk with Orlena came, but it left Jenelle

wholly unsatisfied as well as bewildered. Orlena appeared as cool and aloof as ever and declined to see her brother, though Norman had asked about her. "I have homework to do," she had said with a toss of her brown head."

Once in her room, however, Orlena didn't even open her books. Instead she sat down near the open window and thought. Her brother's injury had shaken her up more than she cared to admit even to herself. For, though she had hidden the feeling for so long and scarcely knew it was there, deep down in her inmost heart was a love for the only kin she had left. True, it was only a small flame, not much more than a flicker, but those long hours she had spent only the day before in school, wondering if Norman had died, had fanned the flame a little higher, and only a little more was needed to ensure that, though it might smolder at times, the flame of love for her brother would never fully die out.

With a sigh, she opened her history and tried to read. When a low knock on her door sounded an hour later announcing supper, she closed her book with the realization that she was still on the same page. Her mind had wandered.

Supper that night was served in the house for the first time in many days, but it was a silent meal with Norman asleep upstairs. Orlena was thankful she didn't have to eat with the men tonight. The quiet of the table suited her mood much better than the talking that would be going on in the bunk house.

"Orlena," Jenelle's quiet voice broke into her young sister's thoughts when supper was over, "I'm going to need you to help with the dishes tonight, unless you would rather take Norman's supper up to him. He would like to see you and you needn't stay long."

"I'll help with the dishes," was the listless reply.

Jenelle and Mrs. O'Connor exchanged glances of surprise, for Orlena's dislike of kitchen chores was well known.

"I believe Orlena is afraid of seeing Norman in bed," Jenelle thought to herself as she watched her sister carry the plates out to the kitchen. She was right. Orlena was afraid. She had never seen anyone injured and in bed before, and the very thought of it sent shivers up her spine. In all her sheltered life, Orlena had scarcely even seen anyone in bed sick. A feeling of revulsion came over her anytime she thought of seeing Norman.

"I wonder if she'll wait to see him until he is out of bed?" This Jenelle wondered as she carried her husband's simple supper to his room.

Orlena did her work in the kitchen without a word save in answer to a question or two from Mrs. O'Connor. Once she was finished, she hurried upstairs and into her room once more.

The following morning Dr. French gave his consent to Norman having visitors, as long as they didn't stay too long and Norman got plenty of rest. Jenelle promised to see to it that the orders were obeyed and the doctor left saying that he would be by later.

"Jenelle," Norman said, as she returned to the bedroom after following the doctor to the stairs, "I must see Hardrich."

"I know. He's waiting downstairs. Now you lie quietly and I'll send him up. But only for a little while," she cautioned with a kiss.

Norman waited somewhat impatiently for the foreman to come. All the time he had been awake he had wondered about the cattle and the other men, but Jenelle wouldn't let him talk long enough to find out anything, and he felt as though he could stand the strain no longer and watched the door anxiously.

Scarcely had Jim Hardrich entered the room, when Norman burst forth, "Hardrich, tell me what happened. What of the cattle? Any men hurt? Did you get them to the train?"

With a chuckle, Hardrich sat down on a chair beside the bed. "Well, we didn't send any men on the train, though we got the cattle to the stockyards and loaded on the train before it pulled out." Then he proceeded to give the information Norman wanted to know in as few and concise words as possible. When he finished, Norman lay quietly for a few minutes before he spoke.

"Thanks, Hardrich. I don't know what the Triple Creek would do without you." His voice was low and his eyes closed for a minute.

Hardrich stood up. "Get some rest now, Mavrich. I'll be by again later, and Hearter wants to see you too."

Norman opened his eyes. "Send him in."

To this Hardrich shook his head. "Not yet. Get some sleep first."

Norman slept for about an hour and when he awoke asked to see Lloyd.

"I'll go call him," Jenelle said. "He's working with Minuet in the corral, just waiting for you to wake up."

"How's Minuet doing?" Norman asked before Jenelle left the room. "I'm afraid it'll be a while before I can ride her." And he looked down at his bandaged leg which lay propped up on a pillow.

"Lloyd can probably tell you better than I can."

Five minutes later, the young hand stepped into the sick room and hesitated in the doorway.

"Come on in, Hearter," Mr. Mavrich said, motioning to the chair beside the bed and holding out his hand.

Lloyd gripped the offered hand and sat down without a word. Nervously he fingered his hat which, in his haste, he had forgotten to leave downstairs; his eyes remained on his dusty boots tapping a soft, uneasy rhythm on the floor.

Norman chuckled. "Come on, Hearter, you act as jumpy as an unbroken horse when he sees the saddle coming. What's bothering you?"

"It's those gates, sir," Lloyd blurted out. "I can't sleep for thinkin' about 'em. I have to help support Mother and the girls even if Connie is teaching, so would you give me a reference and maybe I can get a job on another ranch, though they won't be doing much hirin' these days?" The words came out in a rush.

"A reference? Other ranch? Lloyd Hearter, what are you talking about?" demanded Norman, staring at his visitor.

Lloyd began again. "You see, sir, I know you can't keep someone here who can't follow directions, and if you could give me a reference, some other ranch might . . ."

"I certainly will not give you a reference! Why would I do that?"

The young man who had scarcely slept since the night of the accident didn't raise his eyes and his voice had a slight tremble in it. "It just might help me get another place, sir—"

"Lloyd," Norman spoke firmly. "Answer me one question." Something in the master's tone made Lloyd raise his eyes slowly to meet the steady grey ones before him. "Were those gates latched when you checked them that night?"

"Yes sir."

"That's that then. I won't give you a reference because I can't stand to lose one of my best hands even if it is fall and winter is approaching. So, unless you decide to quit the Triple Creek on your own, you're staying here!"

There was no answer and Norman, seeing that his young hand was unable to speak right then, continued in an earnest voice. "Listen, Hearter. Your life and character are such that had every gate on the ranch been opened that night, I'd never think of blaming you. You have worked faithfully for me since you first came and have earned our trust."

"But sir," Lloyd interrupted, "someone had to have opened those gates. They couldn't have come undone themselves!"

Triple Creek Ranch

CHAPTER 25

PARTIAL SURRENDER

"Right now it doesn't matter who did it or why." Mr. Mavrich paused and put his hand wearily to his head while a look of pain crossed his face.

Seeing it, Lloyd stood quickly. "You should rest now, sir. Thank you. I'll send Mrs. Mavrich up," and turning towards the door, was about to make a hurried departure when Norman's voice halted him.

"Hearter."

"Sir?"

Norman gave a slight smile. "I won't be able to mount a horse for many weeks, the doctor says—" he caught his breath as pain from his injured leg shot through him. "Will you train Minuet?"

"Me, sir? Minuet? Yes, sir!" It was with a feeling of surprise and excitement that Lloyd hurried down the stairs and out to the corral after watching Mrs. Mavrich return to her husband. He felt free. Mr. Mavrich hadn't blamed him and he still had a job. Not only that, but the care and training of the spirited young horse had been entrusted to him.

"Oh, Norman, I shouldn't have let him stay so long," Jenelle whispered, deftly adjusting his pillows and giving him the medicine Dr. French had left. "You aren't strong enough for such long visits yet."

Norman caught her hands in his and looked up into her worried eyes. He smiled gently. "He needed the talk, Sweet. It won't hurt me. He's a fine man and I'd trust him with everything I've got, same as I would with Hardrich."

Bending down, Jenelle kissed him and replied softly, "So would I. Now get some rest, Dear. No more visitors until this afternoon and then only if the doctor agrees."

Wearily Norman closed his eyes. He knew Lloyd hadn't opened those gates and he wondered who had done it. But he didn't wonder for long, for before the watch on his dressing table had ticked sixty seconds away, he was sleeping.

"I don't see why a few more visitors would hurt," Dr. French said thoughtfully. It was mid afternoon and he had just stopped by to see his patient. "It might do him good, as long as he doesn't overdo it. And remember, Mavrich," here the doctor turned to the bed. "There will be no getting out of this bed until I give you leave."

Norman smiled. "There's not much danger of that, Doc. Most of the hard work is done already and the men can handle the everyday chores. They probably won't even miss me much."

The doctor's eyebrows raised slightly and he gave a soft snort. He knew, if Norman didn't, how much the ranch's hired hands were already missing their young, dependable boss.

After the doctor left, Norman had a long line of visitors, for each of the men on the ranch was eager to see him for a few minutes. These continued until the call to supper sent the last of them to the bunk house; and Norman lay back among his pillows enjoying the quietness that comes with the evening. The wind was blowing the curtains softly, causing a gentle stirring of air that caressed his face, while out in the trees the evening twitter and singing of several birds brought a smile to his lips. Everything was so peaceful. If he lay still, his ribs didn't protest and only a faint ache in his leg reminded him of its injury.

When Jenelle came in with the tray of supper, Norman was half asleep. "Would you rather sleep now?" she asked softly.

"Huh?" Turning his head towards the door, Norman opened his eyes. "Oh, I didn't hear you come up. Jenelle, why don't you eat with me. My food will taste twice as good if you are enjoying it with me."

Jenelle wasn't hard to persuade, for she too thought the food tasted better when eaten in the company of her husband. Besides, she wanted a chance to talk with him.

"Jenelle," Norman asked as his wife was placing the empty dishes back on the tray after the meal was over. "Where is Orlena? I haven't seen her since the accident. She isn't sick, is she?"

"No. She just won't come see you. I think she is afraid."

"Of what?"

"Of seeing you in bed. Each time I've mentioned her coming to see you, she gets a frightened look on her face and always has some excuse to offer."

Norman looked troubled. "Are you sure it's seeing me that has made her afraid?"

"What else would she be afraid of?"

When Norman didn't reply, Jenelle, with a puzzled and somewhat thoughtful expression, picked up the tray and carried it out into the hall.

There Mrs. O'Connor met her. "Let me carry that tray. 'Tis not good for you to be doing such work all the time." And before Jenelle could protest, the tray was taken from her hands and she was left to stay or follow as she pleased.

Sunday was a quiet day at Triple Creek Ranch. Hardrich had driven Mrs. O'Connor to church in the morning. Orlena pleaded a headache and declined to go, while Mrs. Mavrich remained behind to look after her husband and Orlena. Mrs. O'Connor had been skeptical about Orlena's headache, but Jenelle could see the pain in her sister's eyes and sympathized with her.

It was late in the afternoon. Norman, having slept most of the day, was feeling better than he had since the accident and was growing restless. All the men of the place were taking full advantage of this day of rest to catch up on much needed sleep after the long, hard days of the round-up, the cattle sorting and the accident, so no one had been by to see Norman all day except his wife, Mrs. O'Connor and Lloyd. At last Norman could stand the stillness and solitude no longer.

"Jenelle!" he called, wondering if she was within hearing.

A moment later, her light footsteps were heard on the stairs and she entered the bedroom.

Norman was trying to sit up in bed, but the pillow kept slipping and with his taped ribs it was difficult to adjust them. In an instant Jenelle was beside the bed and had the pillows fixed and Norman leaned back with a light sigh of contentment.

"I thought you were still sleeping, Dear, or I would have been up sooner," Jenelle apologized. "Is there anything else I can do for you now?"

"How long did the doctor say I had to stay in this bed?"

"He didn't give any certain time, Norman, only that you weren't to get out until he gave you leave."

There was a short silence as Norman stared out the open window. Then turning, he said, "What's Orlena doing?"

"Resting, I think. She's had a headache all day and has scarcely left her room. The poor girl has been so silent since you were hurt; not like herself at all."

Jenelle didn't think that Norman had even heard her reply, for his next question seemed as far from his original question as could be.

"What is Hardrich doing? Think he'll come visit me?"

"Why, I'm sure he will if you want him," Jenelle began, "but—"

"Will you ask him, Sweet?" Norman looked at his wife eagerly. Then, on seeing a look cross her face that he couldn't quite read, he added, "And you come back too. Oh, bother, Jenelle, this bed is making me nervous!" And his restless fingers drummed on the light blanket of the bed.

Laughing, Jenelle promised to return with or without the foreman.

In her room, Orlena lay on her bed with an aching head and argued with her conscience. All day she had felt the pangs of guilt which she never remembered feeling before with such sharpness. "But I didn't open the gates," she told herself for the hundredth time. "I'm not to blame for Norman's accident."

"But the gates wouldn't have opened if you hadn't unlatched them," Conscience replied.

"I wasn't trying to hurt my brother. Why couldn't it have been that Lloyd Hearter fellow who got hurt."

"Would that have made it better?"

"Well, I wish no one had gotten hurt, but why didn't Norman fire Lloyd?"

"You heard what he said yesterday."

She had heard. She had been in her room and had just opened her door to slip outside when Norman's question to Lloyd had arrested her. At first anger had filled her that the hired hand wasn't fired on the spot, but now she couldn't stop thinking. Norman had said it was Lloyd's character and honesty that made him trust him. Even when, to all appearances, he was responsible for the gates being open, his word was still trusted. Would her word be equally trusted? Instinctively she knew it wouldn't. Never before had she cared if she stretched the truth somewhat or even told an out and out lie. The only thing that mattered was that she got what she wanted. But now her conscience told her that was not enough.

"What can I do?" she asked herself with a moan. "Nobody trusts me here. I know they don't. And nobody really loves me either. Why should I stay here where I'm not wanted?"

"You just want to run away before anyone finds out what you did," Conscience accused.

"They'd hate me if they found out! They'd send me away!"

"Isn't that what you want?"

Orlena thought about it. Did she really want to leave this, her only home? Where would she go if she left? The only place she could think of was Madam Viscount's and Norman had already said that he didn't want his sister to turn out like the graduates from that seminary. For some reason, unknown to herself, Norman's approval was becoming important to her. Oh, what was she to do? She couldn't tell what she had done, yet she had lived the last few days in constant fear that her brother would find out. This fear grew when she discovered that Lloyd wasn't blamed for it.

As evening drew on, the cooling breeze blew stronger and the door of her room, which Jenelle hadn't fastened all the way, blew open softly and voices from across the hall came distinctly to the ears of the young, tormented, heartsick girl on the bed. Norman was speaking.

"She wasn't taking care of the chickens. I looked; they had already been taken care of. I didn't think of it though, until I talked with Lloyd yesterday."

Orlena sat up suddenly. She hardly dared to breathe.

There was a soft murmur of voices in reply and Orlena strained her ears. Then Norman spoke again.

"I'm not going to say anything. She was no doubt attempting to get even with Lloyd, for it's no secret that she hasn't liked him from the moment she arrived, but I'm sure she didn't realize what harm could have happened. She doesn't know cattle and what they might do."

Another voice said something in low, deep tones and Orlena guessed Mr. Hardrich was there.

"Don't say anything to anyone. Lloyd knows I trust him. But let's keep praying for Orlena."

With a sudden burst of tears, Orlena threw herself upon her pillow and cried as though her heart would break. Never had she seen or understood a love that would overlook such a fault as hers! The sudden realization that her brother must love her or he would never have said what he did completely overwhelmed her and her sobs grew louder.

At the sound of Orlena's sobs, Jenelle, turning a startled face for a moment to her husband, hurried across to the girl's room. There she tried to comfort her and discover the source of her grief, but in vain, for Orlena couldn't talk.

When the crying continued, Norman threw back the blanket and with a face full of concern, made as though to rise, but Hardrich firmly pushed him back against the pillows.

"You aren't to get up," he reminded him.

"I don't care," Norman replied. "My sister needs me."

"Stay there, and I'll get Jenelle," Hardrich ordered.

"I don't want Jenelle. I want Orlena!"

Promising to see what he could do, Hardrich hurried across the hall and spoke a few words to Mrs. Mavrich.

"Orlena," Jenelle begged, "go to Norman or he'll get out of bed and come here, and you know the doctor said he wasn't to leave his bed. Please, Dear."

"He doesn't want me," sobbed the girl.

"But he does," Jenelle pleaded. "He wants you so much he's willing to injure his leg again to come to you."

This plea seemed to reach Orlena's mind, for with sobs still shaking her and tears streaming down her face, she got up and dashed, half blinded into her brother's room where she flung herself on the bed beside him.

For a moment the only sounds to be heard were the deep, heart wrenching sobs of Orlena. Norman, too moved to say anything at first, could only pull his sister closer and stroke her brown curls. At last he could command his voice enough to speak, though his words were so low that they only reached the ears of the girl beside him.

"It's all right, Orlena. Please stop crying. Oh, Sis, if we only could have learned to love each other early on, perhaps we wouldn't have had so many disagreements. I love you, Sis. I know it hasn't always seemed that way to you, but I do. I'll always love you. You are the only earthly family tie besides Jenelle that is left. Mother and Father, Grandmother and Uncle, all gone. Oh, Orlena, can't you believe I love you!"

In muffled tones, with a choking voice, Orlena gasped out, "You can't love me. Not after what I did!"

"I still love you, Sis."

"But . . . but I unlatched those gates and you could have been killed, and I'm so horrid and no one loves me!" The last ended in another passionate burst of tears.

Standing in the doorway, Jenelle watched with her own eyes full of tears. When the last cry came from the once proud and demanding girl, she could watch no longer but hurried across the room and dropping to her knees beside the bed, put her arms around her sister and husband. "But we do love you, Orlena. We do!" And her own hot tears dropped down to mix with the others on the pillow.

"Orlena," Norman said presently as the slight frame grew quieter and the sobs lessened, "listen to me a minute."

Orlena drew a quivering breath and lay still, feeling Jenelle's arm about her and her brother's hand gently smoothing her hair.

"Jenelle and I will always love you, no matter what you have done. You're family. But there is Someone else who loves you far more than we do. Someone who died that we might be forgiven of our sins. Oh, Sis, if you would only come to Jesus and ask Him to forgive you and help you, your life would be so much easier. You can't really live without Him."

A long silence followed and then Orlena said, her voice still muffled by her hands, "Norman, do you forgive me for unlatching the gates?"

"Yes, Orlena, I do. I forgive you fully."

Drawing a long, shuddering breath, Orlena relaxed. She was completely worn out. For several minutes she didn't move, but lay soaking in the tender love of the brother and sister she had for so long rejected and pushed from her.

Later that night, as she lay in bed, her head still throbbing but her heart delighting in the new love opened to her, she thought back on her past life and resolved to be different. "I will change," she thought, "I won't be so hard to live with and everyone will love me." Norman's words came again to her mind but she pushed them away. She didn't need anyone to help her to be good. If she could be mean and horrid on her own, she could be kind and helpful on her own. They would see.

In their own room, Jenelle was kneeling beside the bed, her hands clasped in those of her husband while she looked into his grey eyes. "Norman, she still needs our prayers as much as ever. If she would only come to the one place of sure rest and true love, her life would be different."

"I know," Norman agreed with a sigh. "I thought perhaps she would, but there is still too much self to give in. It may be a long road ahead, for her and for us, but let's not give up. I felt more compassion for her today than I ever have before. Let's pray for her right now."

T

And now, a sneak preview of Book Two in the
Triple Creek Ranch series:

The trio in the carriage were quiet as Lloyd headed the horse towards the main street of Rough Rock. The sun was well down in the west, and Norman knew it would be dusk when they arrived home. He hoped Jenelle wouldn't start to worry.

"I expect we'll have snow before long," Gregory remarked from the back seat. Though he had been christened Zachariah Gregory, he was nearly always called Greg by those who knew him. And the name seemed to suit him.

A sudden shout startled the men, and instinctively Lloyd drew rein to see what it was about. A showily dressed man had moved away from the saloon and now took a staggering step towards the carriage. "There he is," the man shouted, pointing a finger at Greg. "He's sa man that broke my nose! I'll jus' see how he likes havin' no nose s'tall." His words were a bit slurred and it was obvious that he had been drinking. Reaching down, he began to draw his gun when a sharp voice, cracking like a whip stopped him.

"Don't touch that gun, Con Blomberg, or you'll have me to reckon with."

Blinking, the man turned to stare somewhat stupidly at the men in the front seat of the carriage. "Whoshe dat?" He asked of the men who had stopped and were gathering about to watch the showdown.

"That's Norman Mavrich, Blomberg. I reckon you'd

223

better leave well enough alone," one man told him, taking his arm and trying to lead him back into the saloon. "You can't fight him, especially not when you're half drunk."

"You let go my arm," Blomberg snarled. "I ain't 'fraid a Norman Mavrish an' I ain't drunk. Jesh took a bit a shomething fer the pain. Jesh fer the pain." Then he repeated, "I ain't 'fraid a Norman Mavrish."

"Well, he ought to be," muttered one of the bystanders to another who nodded in agreement.

The half drunk man took a step closer and moved his hand towards his gun belt. Without a word Norman held out his hand to Lloyd. The young hand drew his six-shooter and handed it to him. Normally Norman Mavrich would have had his own gun strapped to his side, but he had left the ranch in such a hurry that he hadn't even thought of it.

"Blomberg," Norman's sharp voice again arrested the man. "Don't touch that gun."

In the silence that followed his words, everyone heard the soft click of the six-shooter in Mr. Mavrich's hand. "If you try to draw that gun, Blomberg, I'll have no choice but to shoot it out of your hand."

Made in the USA
Charleston, SC
29 May 2014